Quiet Room

Book I
Psychotherapy with Ghosts

Joseph S. Covais

NewLink Publishing
2021

Henderson, NV 89002
info@newlinkpublishing.com

Quiet Room

Joseph S. Covais
Copyright © 2021
All rights reserved

Contact the publisher at info@newlinkpublishing.com

Line/Content Editor: Summer Gull/Dave Hardin
Interior Design: Jo A. Wilkins
Cover: Richard Draude

p. cm. — Joseph S. Covais / Paranormal
Copyright © 2021/ Joseph S. Coavis
All Rights Reserved

ISBN: 978-1-948266-18-5/Paperback
ISBN: 978-1-948266-30-7/E-Pub

1. Fiction / Ghost
2. Fiction / Fantasy / Paranormal
3. Fiction / Fantasy / Romantic

NewLink Publishing
Henderson, NV 89002
Info@newlinkpublishing.com
Published and printed in the United States of America

1 2 3 4 5 6 7 8 9 0

For Donna.
You always said we should write a book together.
We have — this is it.

ACKNOWLEDGMENTS

There are some people whose help and advice in this Psychotherapy With Ghosts adventure can't go unacknowledged. I list them here in no particular order, but if I've left your name out, forgive me – you know who you are:

Margaret King
Tobin Jordan
Eli Windover
Adelicia Vander Els
Jessica Lovely, George and Kathy Bevis
Dave Hardin, my editor at Mystic

Thanks. You guys are the best.

Quiet Room

Chapter 1

Summer, 1970

David Weis closed his Manhattan psychotherapy practice and a few weeks later took title to a remote property on Lake Champlain—a house, barn, and carriage building, the last remnants of what had once been a proud estate. His parents advised against it. His girlfriend too. Even the realtor told him the buildings weren't worth salvaging because the only value was in the land.

The house was old. He guessed at least one hundred and fifty years, probably more. David liked that. The Doric columns, gable returns, and low-pitched roof in particular. All were features of architecture which announced the optimism of a new republic—one founded on classical ideals. But it was a more personal sense of coming home—the distinct impression that for a long time, this place had been waiting for him, and him alone. That's what really drove the sale.

The entire building was fascinating, but one room in particular drew him. Second floor, north-east corner. On first inspection, the room seemed like it had been used for decades as mere storage space. Discarded furniture and other household fixtures were stacked to the ceiling. After two days of steady work, David emptied it. Revealed was a room unspoiled by twentieth century technology. No electrical wiring or telephone line had ever penetrated its walls.

The room's uncorrupted state was a delight in itself, but the walls adorned with frescoes were an unforeseen bonus. At waist height

1

was a continuous decoration of ochre-brown, life sized Grecian urns connected by swags of green laurel. It was something one might see at Pompeii or Herculaneum.

Having this room, with all its intact ideals, was like retrieving a piece of the distant past, and to David the past was better than the present.

In the following weeks David returned and returned to the Quiet Room, as he now called it. He found the simplicity, cleanliness, and order calming. The room remained on his mind as he explored storage lofts, attics, and closets throughout the property. Sometimes he found items which looked like they could have been part of the original furnishings. These he cleaned and placed inside.

An over-the-mantel mirror found in the attic fit nicely above the fireplace. He flanked it with a pair of brass candlesticks, also from the attic. Holes in the plaster matched the brackets of three whale-oil lamps found in the barn. David cleaned and remounted them.

A small room adjoined the Quiet Room. It would only have been large enough to admit a bed and bureau in the past, but in the present was filled with detritus instead. Under piles of crates and boxes he found a klismos chair. It had a caned seat with a black lacquered finish and gold pin striping. A spray of colorful flowers were painted across the back panel.

He brought the chair into the Quiet Room. It looked the most natural positioned by the north-facing window.

At day's end, David sat on the windowsill to have a cigarette and watch twilight come on. He contemplated the room and events which had brought him to this place—a patient's suicide, Dr. Koenigsberg's advice, a sleepless night followed by an impulsive road trip, at the end of it had stood a "For Sale" sign.

On this particular night, the moon rose full. Bright enough to read by. Crickets were everywhere, chirping like mad. He supposed there could be a million, ten million of them between himself and the lake. It was impossible to guess, but he stayed at the window, deep in thought until well after darkness fell.

Time slipped away.

Chapter 2

May 1838

Acrid whiffs of smoke and charred wood hung in the streets of Burlington. With every breath, Daniel's throat felt raw. He must have inhaled too much of it, maybe some sparks too.

Toward the city, a black smudge rose from among the buildings. He recalled an angry mob, torches, fighting. Somebody had knocked him down. The roof collapsed. Someone had dragged him out of the burning rubble, bless them.

A well-dressed gentleman came down the gang plank, followed by a drayman carrying his bags.

"I'm Hamilton," he said. "The livery sent you?"

"It did, sir. I'm to take you to the Pomeroy House."

"Very good." He moved to step into the buggy but stopped short. "Good God, young man. You look as if you've been half roasted."

"Yes, half roasted, very nearly, sir."

"What the devil happened to you?" Hamilton inspected his singed clothing and swollen burns.

The irony of the statement wasn't lost. Daniel smiled. "The church was on fire."

"The Catholic church?" Hamilton climbed into the buggy.

"Yes sir. Last night, a mob set it on fire."

"Deplorable," said Hamilton with disgust. "There's no excuse for burning churches."

"Yes, sir, deplorable. I tried to help put the fire out and got burned."

"I should say you did."

The wharves were crowded with cargo, wagons, and activity of all kinds. Daniel backed up the buggy and turned it toward the city, wending through crowded streets and narrow passages.

"I think you've driven me before," said Hamilton. "What was your name? I don't remember it."

"Daniel Dwyer, sir. And yes, I did drive for you once. It was in March, I think."

"Well Dwyer, you handle a horse well."

"Thank you. I love horses. My dad told me, 'Danny, every horse will tell you how it likes to be handled. All you have to do is listen.'"

Hamilton gave his own, horse-like snort.

"Like this one here. She's an old livery nag. She don't like to be hurried and she don't like to turn left. Who knows why, but if you remember that, she'll work all day."

"Perhaps. I bought a new horse last month. The deuced animal is most obstinate. A beautiful Morgan, but with the heart of a mule. He refuses to be in harness."

"Well sir, being in harness is not always easy for a proud animal like a horse."

Over the following two days, Daniel drove Hamilton to appointments throughout the city. Judging from the questions he asked, it seemed Mr. Hamilton took an interest in him.

"How old are you?"

"Sixteen, sir, nearly seventeen."

"Have you no family?"

"No sir, no family, sir."

"You are a Catholic. You pray to their idols?"

"I pray to the saints, yes, and the Virgin Mary, and the Lord, just as anyone else."

"Your devotion is admirable," said Hamilton. "I haven't prayed in a long time."

On the morning of the third day, Daniel brought the gentleman to the docks.

"Well, Dwyer," he said, taking a silver dollar from his vest. "You've been a fine fellow. Take this," he told him. "Those boots of yours were ruined in that fire. Buy yourself a pair that aren't crumbling apart."

4

Hamilton held out the large silver coin, but something made Daniel hesitate. "It's a tip, my boy. You've done excellent work for me these last few days. Take it."

An inner voice told him to take a chance.

"Thank you for your kindness, sir, but I'd rather earn it. I want a better job. If I had your mark on a letter vouching for me, I know I could get one with that."

Hamilton leaned back, eyes assessing, scrutinizing, appraising.

"You know everyone, Mr. Hamilton. Everyone respects you. It would be a great help."

"Where did you say you were from?"

"Halifax, sir. I came here looking for work, but all they tell me is, sorry son, times are hard."

The gentleman tapped Daniel's chest with the head of his walking stick. "Listen, young man," he said. "I have a proposal. If you want a job working on my property you can return with me. I need a young fellow with a strong back who can handle horses."

Hamilton pulled two more dollars from his vest. "You have initiative, Dwyer. I like that. Take this money. If you decide to go, come back wearing a pair of heavy boots and clothes that aren't burned full of holes. This steamer for Willsborough leaves at one thirty. If you're not aboard, then spare yourself the indignity of charity. Donate the money to rebuild your papist church."

"New boots and clothes. That's very generous of you, sir."

"Don't worry. I'll see that you work for them."

At Willsborough, an old man with a buggy waited near the dock.

"Sandborne," Hamilton called. "This is Daniel. I've brought him to help us for the summer and to break that mule of a horse."

"Very good, sir." The old gent shook Daniel's hand but otherwise said little on the three-mile trip to the property.

"You'll stay with Sandborne in the carriage house," Hamilton explained as they approached the residence.

Daniel thought the Hamilton home looked like that of a rich man; white, with tall columns in front. He'd always wondered what the people who lived in such houses were like. Now he would find out.

"Sandborne," Hamilton said. "Get the boy situated and when you're done, bring him to me and Mrs. Hamilton."

Daniel followed Sandborne to the carriage house. Though the old man walked with a limp, he easily climbed up a steep stair to the loft. There was a stove, a couple of trundle beds, and a few sparse furnishings. A mirror hung on the wall opposite a print of General William Henry Harrison.

"You can put your things by that bed there, son," said Sandborne.

Except for a change of clothing, his Bible, and a toothbrush there wasn't much for Daniel to put away. Still, thanks to Mr. Hamilton he wore the first decent suit of clothes he'd had in years and boots he bought from the widow of a dead man.

"What are they like, the Hamiltons?" he asked.

"The Hamiltons are a nice family. I've worked for them a long time. The gentleman can be very exacting, but he's a good man and you'll find him fair."

It felt forward, asking more, but the sudden turn his life was taking drove Daniel's curiosity on. "Does anyone else live here?"

"Yes. There's Mrs. Hamilton of course, and their daughter. There's the housemaid too. Most of the time you and I will take our meals in the kitchen with her. We keep a small flock of sheep here and a pair of milk-cows. This summer Mr. Hamilton wants the buildings repainted, new fences put up, and help with this new horse."

Sandborne stopped and appraised the boy. "Come," he said. "You look like you need something to eat. Am I right?"

At the house, Daniel was ushered into the kitchen. From elsewhere in the building came the sound of piano progressions. The start, stop, and restart told him someone was practicing. The kitchen was warm, full of the smell of baking bread and stew. His stomach growled. At the cook stove a young girl of perhaps twelve or thirteen stirred a pot.

"Julia," said Sandborne. "This is Daniel."

She offered no more than a glance over her shoulder at the introduction.

George Hamilton and his wife came in.

"Gloriana," he said. "This is the boy I told you about."

The gentleman's wife was a handsome woman with dark made up hair. Her dress held a somber, deep plum color.

Hamilton invited him to take a seat at the table.

"Let me see those burns," the lady said, her voice soft. Daniel recognized it as the voice of someone resisting the urge to cough.

Daniel watched her manicured hands glide over his abrasions. She directed the housemaid to get some clean rags, soap, and a basin of water.

Mrs. Hamilton looked at him with pity in her eyes. Patches of his skin were inflamed, swollen, scabbing over. "This will hurt a little," she said. She washed his wounds and applied a salve of comfrey to his scorched arms, hands, and face. She wound a bandage around the worst of it.

"Are you hungry, son?" asked Hamilton.

Daniel nodded, disoriented by all the kindness being extended.

The lady told the housemaid to bring a bowl of lamb-stew with bread and butter.

Devouring the best meal he'd eaten that year, Daniel could hear the Hamiltons talking in the hallway.

"He's a poor boy...hard worker...initiative," Mr. Hamilton said. "Knows horses too...mob burned down the Catholic church...miserable louts, nearly killed him."

"But George, what'll we do with him?"

"...stay the summer...help Sandborne. When winter comes he can move on."

Daniel dipped the bread crust into the bowl, soaking up broth until he felt someone's eyes on him. He looked up to see a young girl in a coral necklace standing at the threshold, one ivory hand resting flat against the door jam. She had the deepest shade of brown hair, and her eyes were startlingly gray.

"I'm sorry. I've been staring," she said.

"It's alright, miss, I don't mind."

Chapter 3

Summer, 1970

Time flew and summer was almost at an end. Except for the weekly long-distance call to his girlfriend, several days would pass without a conversation with another human being. That might have bothered most people, but David liked it. Overall, he felt more at ease, steadier on the gun. Except for one thing. A growing impression that someone else was in the house. Not just anywhere, but in the Quiet Room.

The first time he took notice was about a month after he'd moved in. That evening, while drying plates at the kitchen sink, David kept looking up at the fluorescent light on the ceiling, above which was the Quiet Room. Something kept drawing his attention that way. It was eerie.

Once the room had been cleaned out and antiques placed inside, the phenomena came more frequently. It seemed stronger too. One night, while David looked for a notebook he was pretty sure he'd left upstairs, he ran up the back staircase. From there it was an automatic, easy turn into the Quiet Room, but David stopped short. An undeniable sensation told him someone was in there.

His heart raced with apprehension, but he had enough resolve to take a step forward. What else could he do?

The floor creaked and David froze. He finally peeked around the corner. The Quiet Room was lit, very dimly, but without question.

With his heart pounding in his chest, he grabbed a spackle knife from a stepladder just within reach and called, "Who's there?"

Nothing. No answer.

"Is there someone in there?"

No response.

David lunged to the doorway—putty knife held high.

What he saw slammed him with disbelief and fear. A transparent woman sat sewing on a transparent sofa. David held up his hand as if he could stop the vision, then retreated, his back to the wall and his mouth agape. Yes, it was clearly a woman's silhouette. Not solid, but there. She was setting a needle, then pulling it through until the thread was taut, over and over. The image flickered and the Quiet Room went dark.

Back downstairs, David snatched a bottle of slivovitz from the kitchen counter and poured a coffee mug half full, forgoing ice. As he drank, the cool burn in his throat grounded him in physical reality. He kept the lights on, and his eyes fixed on the stairs. Maybe he'd been inhaling too many fumes with all this remodeling. Polyurethane, paint thinner. That stuff can't be good for you, he thought.

Stress does things to people too, he reminded himself. Maybe it was stress that brought this on. Cheryl Jankowsky's suicide, quitting his psychotherapy career, moving up-state—it would have been a lot for anyone.

Except David felt convinced that were he to climb the staircase and turn the corner, the specter would be there, sitting, sewing...waiting.

In the morning he went back and cautiously looked around. The putty knife still lay on the floor where he'd dropped it and ran, but otherwise everything was in order; serene and undisturbed.

Nonetheless, every few nights the feeling returned. David tried to ignore it, tried to tell himself it wasn't there, but it didn't work. Tonight, it returned again, persistent and stronger than ever before. He stood at the foot of the stairs, staring up into the darkness.

These events had to be faced, he told himself. Confrontation wasn't his thing, but David had reached the conclusion that whoever or whatever this phenomenon was, it wasn't aggressive and probably not dangerous.

Wielding a steak-knife from the kitchen drawer as a precaution, David climbed the stairs slowly, waiting several seconds on each succeeding tread.

At the top, sliding forward inch by inch, he advanced until he saw the open doorway to the Quiet Room. The light from inside was particularly bright, the play of shadows in the hall betraying movement inside.

David inched forward until he could see part of the figure. He took the moment to study what he saw. A woman's left shoulder and arm, a wisp of dark hair as well, and a basket on the cushion beside her.

He waited, crouched in the dark, silently observing her for nearly an hour. Once she reached into her basket. He saw the flash of a hand and for an instant, part of a face. Finally, it was time to stand and confront the stranger in his house.

From the doorway he could see her fully. The young woman seated on the daybed was dressed in the fashion of a long, long time ago. Her blue dress had a fitted bodice, with a wide, scooped neck and very tight sleeves. From beneath the hem of her voluminous skirt, one of her feet dangled over the edge of the divan, suggesting that her other leg was folded beneath her. The shoe reminded him of a ballet slipper.

She raised her head. "I see you are there waiting, sir. Do you wish to speak to me?" The controlled voice lacked agitation or excitement.

"Who are you? What are you doing here?" David demanded from the doorway. "What is your name?"

"I am Almira Hamilton. I live here."

David studied her more carefully. The beautiful young woman had a crown of dark hair. It looked oiled, center parted, with long spiral curls dangling from her temples. An ornate silver comb held a braided knot in place, while a necklace of beaded coral was fastened around her throat. Her pale gray eyes accentuated her other delicate, even features. All these things he could plainly see.

"Then," he ventured, "you can see me?"

She looked perplexed by his questions. "Of course. But, sir, before we converse more, don't you think we should be properly introduced?"

The response took him off guard. "Excuse me," he said. "I'm sorry. My name is Doctor David Weis."

She seemed delighted by his answer, clapping her hands together. "A physician. I knew you were a gentleman."

"Well, not an ordinary physician," he hastened to explain. "I'm a

11

doctor who tries to heal troubled people with conversation."

"Then you must be a doctor of divinity. A minister?"

"No, not that," he said. "More a doctor of philosophy. Psychology to be specific."

"Whichever it is, Doctor Weis, please do take a seat and visit with me."

Clearly the knife wasn't needed. David slipped it into his hip pocket and entered the room. Crossing the threshold felt like leaving one world and stepping into another—hers. The room itself seemed to be part of her manifestation. The daybed she sat on and the pictures on the wall weren't there before, at least not in David's time. The whale oil lamps which he knew held no oil, were now lighted, and there was a bed of coals glowing in the fireplace. Odd, he thought, no heat.

"Please take a chair."

He reached for the klismos chair and placed it near the center of the room. "What are you reading?"

"*The Young Lady's Friend.*"

"And what does it say?"

"This book says that man is woman's physical protector and woman, man's moral protector. It is a beautiful idea. I cling to it. Is that foolish of me, to cling to a beautiful idea?"

"No, I don't think it's foolish at all, but beautiful in itself."

This person was different. Her mannerisms and inflections were archaic, and she held assumptions to which he was unaccustomed. Yet, infused with so much of her youth, these qualities seemed fresh and ordinary.

Time passed, dreamlike. David felt lost in their conversation about how much she loved to read her collections of novels and stories from Greek mythology. Her favorite was the tale of Andromeda and Perseus.

"I'm not acquainted with that story."

"Then allow me to inform you," she said with excitement. "Princess Andromeda was the daughter of Cepheus and Cassiopeia. Her mother's pride in her daughter's beauty offended the gods—it was boastful. As punishment, she was forced to offer Andromeda as a sacrifice to Poseidon. She was chained to a rock at the seashore and left to be ravaged. In the end, Andromeda is rescued by the noble Perseus. She becomes his bride. I have read it a thousand times."

As she told the story, his mind drifted. Was she a dream, hallucination, or a glimpse into a supernatural, spirit world he had rejected long ago? He almost posed the question to her but she spoke again.

"Doctor," she said. "I have enjoyed our conversation so much. You will be my new interlocutor, won't you? I warn you though, mine is a lonely life, and I am sometimes plagued by melancholy."

"That's alright." David answered as he would have back in his Manhattan office. "Many people feel that way. It's not unusual to be sad sometimes. It's ordinary."

"But I have no ordinary sadness, Dr. Weis." She yawned. "Please excuse me, I feel so tired." Even as she said these words she faded, her transparency shimmering before vanishing, daybed and all.

From the klismos chair David looked around at the now empty room. He had a heightened awareness of his surroundings; the sun rising over the mountains across the lake and the clean, cold hearth. He likened it to emerging from hypnosis.

Dumbfounded, David considered and reconsidered how astonishing this had all been. Had it been a dream? A hallucination? Maybe playing around with psychedelics all those years ago had induced the whole experience. Maybe this was just a bad trip.

His mind went back to Almira Hamilton. She didn't seem so different from patients he'd had who were isolated, disoriented, or depressed. You would, he thought, conduct psychotherapy in the same way with such a person, even if they were a ghost. Wouldn't you? Why would this be any different?

"Psychotherapy with ghosts," he said aloud, laughing.

Chapter 4

Summer, 1970

With his ladder propped against the nearest apple tree Daniel climbed to the top. From this elevation he could see most of the Hamilton property— the stately white house, the barn and carriage house closer to him in the orchard, vegetable and flower gardens in between. The farm lane a few yards behind him led to Lake Champlain. If he craned his neck, he saw glimpses of blue water sparkling in the sunlight. It all looked and felt like home, for such it had become over the last eighteen months. Thanks be to God. His struggles to keep a roof over his head and his stomach from growling with hunger now seemed a long way off.

Redirecting his attention, Daniel saw Mrs. Hamilton and Almira exit the house, arm in arm. It was their habit whenever the two were together out of doors. Even without their bonnets, at this distance it was hard to tell them apart, except that one of them stopped frequently to cough into a handkerchief. Mrs. Hamilton, always weak and short of breath, seldom went on excursion of any kind since he'd come to live with them.

Consumption was upon her. To him it was obvious, though he, nor anyone else, ever spoke it aloud. His own mother had lingered on for years before receiving her heavenly reward. Daniel could only pray this kind woman's suffering would be brief.

"Good day Mrs. Hamilton, and you too, Miss Almira," he called as they came near.

"Daniel, I see you've been hard at work."

"That I have, ma'am. There's six-bushel baskets already full and I'm not yet half finished picking."

"Dolly," said Mrs. Hamilton to her daughter. "Do find a clean spot to place my cushion. I need to rest."

There was a nice location in the sun. Almira led her mother to it, eased her to the ground and approached the ladder. How he secretly loved her, worshiped her, adored and was captivated by her.

"Aren't you afraid to be so high up?" she asked.

"Goodness no, miss, not if the ladder is steady." Moments like this were precious to him. "Would you like an apple, miss? I see one here that's perfectly ripe."

"Yes, please."

Daniel twisted the apple from the stem and came down a few rungs to hand it to her. Almira's sweet voice, her gentle, reaching hand, and expectant bright eyes as she took it from him were intoxicating.

He climbed the rest of the way to the ground and repositioned the ladder.

"Have I told you, Papa said he would buy me a pony for my birthday," said Almira as she took the first bite.

"I didn't know you could ride."

"I can't, not yet. But he says you did such a splendid job training Marcus and the new horse, that he might have you teach me."

The thought of having reason to be with Almira, being near her, instructing her, guiding her movements, was a thrill.

"I probably shouldn't have said anything, but would you teach me?"

"Dolly," called Mrs. Hamilton. "Come help me up. I can go further now."

Almira looked toward her mother, who'd begun coughing, then back at him. "I have to go," she said.

They left, arm in arm, but not back to the house. Instead, they continued further down the lane. Daniel knew their destination, a small private cemetery hidden in a grove of trees.

Chapter 5

Summer, 1970

The following weekend David sat in his truck, waiting at the depot, thinking. Angela's bus would arrive any minute. He'd met her at a bar last summer. She turned out to be a graduate student in American Literature and Library Science. She was smart, really smart. She was attractive, and on the pill too, so sex wasn't a problem.

Angela was uninhibited about sex. He liked that. She wasn't afraid to initiate things either. He liked that too. And like a lot of Italian girls he'd known, she had a subtle sarcasm woven into most of what she said. He found it playful and kind of sexy, even if he was often the target of those remarks.

David reflected on his thought process. He found it natural to analyze people in this way, reduce them to their component parts, tally up their faults and virtues, even Angela. Sometimes it bothered him to think so clinically. It was such a detached and lousy way to relate to people.

Notwithstanding, he genuinely looked forward to the visit. Between work at the library and her city college night classes, it was difficult for Angela to get away for several days at one stretch. This year Columbus

Day fell on a Sunday, and a lot of establishments were taking the following day off. The yellow, red, and bright orange scenery made it the perfect time for her first visit. Even if the house was still in a great deal of disrepair.

Passengers stepped down from the bus. Angela's straight, black hair held back in a long ponytail and an ever present, enormous handbag slung over her shoulder made her easy to identify. Smiling, she turned his way. He walked toward her and pressed a kiss on her lips It felt good to feel her in his arms again.

"How was your trip?"

"Endless," she said. "God, you're way the hell up here. But I'm here now, right?"

After the driver unloaded the luggage, David grabbed her bag and pointed. "We're in that white truck over there."

"You weren't lying. You really did buy a pickup truck." Angela laughed. "You've gone redneck on me. Did it come with an Elect Wallace bumper sticker?"

"No, but that's not a bad idea."

Once she and her bag were in the cab of the truck, he took her to eat at the town's only diner. Before heading to the house, they paid a visit to the supermarket and liquor store.

"I still can't believe you bought a pickup truck. I've never ridden in one of these. What a gas. This thing is a riot."

"Hey, I've still got the Ghia, but up here I need a truck, something that can haul stuff and has good heat. The Ghia just didn't cut it."

Rounding a turn, Angela got her first view of the property a hundred yards ahead. "That's it, isn't it." she said.

"How could you tell?"

"It's got your name all over it. Remote. Set off by itself."

"And a little run down," David added.

"I wasn't going to mention that, but since you brought it up, yes."

Tires crunched on the gravel driveway. She brought her face near

18

the windshield to see the house better.

"Christ, David, this place is huge."

"Well, don't get too excited," he warned. "It's still pretty rough on the inside."

The sun set early at this time of year, so it was best to show her the property before they took a tour of the inside. Parking behind the house, they got out. David took her hand and gestured toward the buildings around them.

"So, this one here is the carriage house. That's where the Ghia is right now, but I'm going to set up the antique shop there. It needs a paint job, like everything here, but it's really in good shape."

"Now, over here," he said in the style of a tour-guide, "is the barn. It's a little rougher I'd say, but it's probably the oldest building here, older than the house."

"When do you think this place was built?" Angela asked.

"As far as I can tell, sometime around 1830."

Angela arched an eyebrow. "That's pretty old."

He knew she meant this as a point of concern, but to him, the age of the building was an appealing asset. He led her past the barn and down an overgrown farm lane.

"Over on this side is an old apple orchard. It's been left un-tended for God knows how long. All these trees need to be pruned, but I've gotten some nice apples out of here anyway."

David walked up to the nearest tree and pulled off a ripe one.

"They taste better than they look." He took a bite and held it out to her. She took a bite too.

"Now, if you go farther along this lane it goes down to the lake. It's really, really nice down there. I'll show you tomorrow. Right now, let's go back so you can see the house."

They went in through the kitchen at the back of the building. The screen door slammed behind them. Angela looked around at the appliances. She commented on the glass-fronted cabinets.

19

"Except for this old linoleum flooring, the kitchen looks pretty good," he said. "What do you think?"

Angela had to agree. Inspecting the remodeled bathroom, her slow "hmmm" indicated a favorable reaction. So far, so good, he thought. David took her into the central hallway. At the front door he pointed to the narrow panes of glass surrounding it.

"At the time this house was built these windows were called lights. They brighten the whole central part of the building. Now, come in here. I'm pretty sure this was the old parlor. Don't you love these windows, the way they go all the way from the ceiling to the floor? And the front room on the other side is the same."

David led her to another room situated behind the parlor. "I think this room might have been a library or office. It has all these cool built-in bookcases. Anyway, as you can tell, I put my office in here."

He showed her the primitive surface wiring and push-button light switches. "This all has to come out," he told her. "I don't even like to use it. I don't trust it." They stepped carefully over an extension cord running all the way from the kitchen. Stepladders, cans of paint, paint stripper, brushes, and rollers were scattered across the newspaper-covered floor.

David led her back to the central staircase. The bannister was smooth, the edges of the steps worn down from decades of use.

"Don't lean on that railing too much," David said. "It's a little rickety. In fact, it's better to use the back staircase. It's a lot safer, but today we can make an exception."

The upstairs rooms were in worse shape. Ceilings sagged in two of them, and one room had a piece of plywood where a window should have been. "I'm thinking a falling tree came through it."

"David," she asked. "Do all of these rooms have fireplaces?"

"Pretty much, yeah, though I wouldn't feel comfortable lighting a fire in them, not yet anyway."

David brought her toward the back of the second floor, saving the

20

best for last.

"Check this out," he said, inviting her to share his secret treasure. "This room is something else."

"Wow, it's like stepping into a different building." Angela circled, inspecting the frescoes adorning the plastered walls. "These were once elegant, even if primitive."

"David, these paintings are like something right out of my art history textbook—they're really gorgeous."

He pointed with obvious pride. "I'm pretty sure there was a basic stencil for the urn and a few different ones for the greenery connecting them."

"Don't tell me. This is your perfect room," she said.

"Actually, I like to call it the Quiet Room, but, yes, you're right."

Angela went to one corner and paced off the perimeter. "This room is really different," she said slowly. "It's got a different vibe. It doesn't feel, I don't know, empty, like the rest of the house. It feels more like someone lives here. That's the only way I can put it. It's strangely beautiful."

"Maybe it's haunted," said David. "Who knows?"

Angela stepped closer. "You know, you're a funny guy. I get that you like this neo-classical thing as an aesthetic style, but what emotional appeal does it have for you?"

"That's easy. There's this naïve optimism—as if man could be perfected through a perfect society. Does that answer your question?"

"No, it doesn't. You avoided the point I was making. I asked about its emotional appeal."

Seconds passed. David liked to think things through before answering. It was a peculiar idiosyncrasy of his, but she'd stopped commenting on it long ago. He liked to think she'd grown fond of it. "Well it's simple. Its innocence is heartbreaking, and there's beauty in that because it evokes a time before the first disappointment."

"Of course," Angela said, with signature understatement. "How obvious. I should have known."

The next day, the lovers got up late. David busied himself running new electrical wiring into the back parlor, mounting outlet boxes to the baseboards. He could hear her in the kitchen, organizing the cabinets and singing along with the transistor radio.

Later in the afternoon, they packed a picnic basket and headed down the dirt lane.

"I'm going to show you this really cool spot. I think it's my favorite place on the whole property," David said.

He took her down the farm lane to an elevation near a stand of trees. The ground was covered in a carpet of summer clover, with an exposed ledge of rock nearby. It seemed natural to observe the landscape from this position.

Angela pointed across the lake. "Is that Vermont on the other side?"

"Yeah, that's Vermont. I think it's the town of Bridport directly across. That peninsula that juts out is called Thompson's Point. I know that much."

"Okay," said Angela. "And how far does your property go?"

"Actually, this is about the end of it. The property line is somewhere between where we are and that cluster of woods over there. It was all one estate originally, but the land got chopped up over the course of time."

He was about to spread an old army blanket on the ground when Angela protested.

"Don't. We can just lie down on the grass," she said, throwing herself to the ground.

David kneeled beside her, admiring her figure. Her middle was exposed, a band of firm olive skin between her faded jeans and a clingy white top. Her long black hair flowed across the deep green clover.

"I like that sweater," he said. "Why don't you take it off…slowly."

Angela's face flushed. "You have animalistic intentions, don't you?"

"A lot of the time, yes." He glided a hand from her hips to her shoulder.

He leaned into her and they kissed, then kissed again, but when David's fingertips started to explore her clothing, she grabbed his wrist.

"Not out here. Someone could be watching."

"Like who?"

"I don't know. Some weirdo. A sex pervert."

David made a show of turning his head in every direction. "I don't see any sex perverts."

"You know what I mean."

He acquiesced. After all, anticipation was part of the excitement. "But once we get back to the house, you're all mine."

"Is that a promise?" Angela said, as she sat up and lit a long cigarette.

David opened a bottle of wine, filled two coffee mugs and handed her one. He swept a hand over the orange and red landscape. "Isn't this place beautiful?"

"Yeah, it is, but Jesus, don't you get bored? I mean, there's nothing up here."

"Not really, no." He shifted position and continued. "Angie, I love it here, and I feel a lot calmer now. It's good for me, certainly from a mental health perspective. I was hoping you'd like it here too."

"It is a beautiful location—I can't argue with that. I guess you got a lot of house for the money, but..."

David beckoned her on with the tilt of his head.

"Well, to tell the truth, I think it's kind of spooky."

In light of recent events, he took note of her comment. "It's just an old building, but it's funny you should say that. Do you believe there could be such a thing as ghosts? Sometimes I think I do."

"Nope." She flicked her cigarette butt. "That's a lot of baloney. This place is getting to you. Think about it. You believe in ghosts, but you don't believe in God. You can't have it both ways."

23

She did have a point; if ghosts were real, and thus the supernatural, why not God as well?

That evening, after making love, they opened another bottle of wine. Angela rummaged in her purse and pulled out a crooked joint. "Hey doctor, look what I brought with me."

David smiled, though he wasn't thrilled. Smoking pot usually made him feel a little paranoid, but Angela liked to get high. This weekend he didn't want anything to come between them.

Now that the room had electricity, she turned on the stereo and tuned in to a music station.

"Johnny Mathis. Now that's real make-out music," she cooed.

Later that night, long after they had gone to sleep, Angela shook him by the shoulder.

"David. David, wake up," she whispered in his ear. "I think there's someone in the house."

"Did you hear something?"

"No, but it feels like someone's upstairs."

He knew what it was, or rather, who it was, but of course didn't dare say anything. "Don't worry. Go back to sleep," he mumbled. "It's only squirrels."

Chapter 6

June, 1840

The front parlor of the Hamilton home was bright as day on spring mornings. Almira sat on the settee stitching an embroidery sampler. Gloriana Hamilton sat beside her, reading the latest issue of Godey's *Lady's Book*. She looked up to monitor her daughter's needlework. Removing the spectacles from her nose, she folded them and rested the magazine on her lap.

As she watched her surviving child, her mind drifted from the sampler to Almira's maturity which, with each passing month, was unfolding into womanhood. She wouldn't be there to guide her through the seasons of life: courtship, marriage, childbirth. Motherless daughters were always at a disadvantage.

"Momma," her daughter said, without looking up from her work, "Daniel says he can give me another riding lesson this afternoon. Do I have your permission?"

"Yes, that will be fine, but mind the time. You must be home by four o'clock." Her voice broke into a short cough. She paused, regained her breath. "Your father returns from Burlington this evening. You'll need to be—here—to receive him."

Before Almira could answer another coughing spell seized Mrs. Hamilton, but this time more violent. Inspecting the handkerchief in her hand, she tried to conceal terror at what she saw. Tiny specks of blood. She was dying of consumption, she knew it. She'd seen this happen to others—her aunt, a childhood friend, people in town.

As Gloriana Hamilton sat gasping for air, Almira poured a tumbler of water at the sideboard. Once in hand, she drank deeply, then wiped a speck of blood from the rim. The floor to ceiling windows of the parlor, open to the world outside, held her attention.

After a few more sips, her thoughts turned to her daughter. No matter how Almira tried to conceal it, it was obvious that she fancied Daniel. Gloriana had noticed her watching him from the window too many times, and there were too many falsely casual questions about him. She knew what those things meant.

"Mirie… Dolly. Daniel is a nice boy but do remember your station. Do you follow me?"

Her daughter nodded automatically.

Gloriana swallowed a bit more water. "Be proper at all times. Mind what you converse about." She took a moment to rest her voice. "If you must dismount, don't do so where the ground is uneven, lest there be reason for you to be handled in a fashion which is unladylike. Do you understand me completely?"

"Of course, I do," Almira promised.

An hour later, Daniel emerged from the barn holding two horses by the reins. One was Marcus, now his horse. The other was Almira's, a smaller, russet-colored pony.

Since living with the Hamiltons he'd grown tall, his shoulders broad. He wore his sandy hair long, all the way to his shirt-collar. A black cravat was tied around his neck, setting off a checkered vest. His gray trousers were tucked into his boots, which were freshly blacked.

Ahead, Almira waited at the mounting stone.

He stepped near. "Is that a new riding habit you have on today, miss?"

"Oh, no." She glanced at her sleeves. "But I have altered it to be more à la mode. Do you like it?"

"It's very nice," said Daniel.

"Mr. Dwyer," she asked. "What shall we do for my second lesson?"

"Well, miss, this afternoon I thought we might take a ride entirely around your father's property. That is, if it suits you."

"Oh," she said with a little bounce on her toes. "It certainly does."

A large cat circled her skirts, its tail pointed upward. Almira scooped it up and nuzzled it affectionately. Daniel watched with envy.

"Wigwam," she said, "you stay here. Momma will return in just a little while."

While Daniel held Ginger Snap's bridle, Almira mounted her horse from the steppingstone.

"Remember miss, as long as you're not frightened, your horse won't be either."

They rode off together—first to the lakeshore, then northward along the heights overlooking the water and the scenery beyond.

"You're doing well," Daniel commented along the way. "Hold the reins more gently, though."

Almira relaxed her grip only momentarily. "But I'm afraid Ginger Snap will bolt."

"She won't," he said. "Not if you remember what I said. She can sense if you're frightened. Horses always can. Try to be relaxed and she will be too."

"I will try," she promised.

Turning west, away from the lake, they followed a farm lane along pastures where sheep grazed, and lazy cows lolled. It delighted Daniel to be in the position of teaching young Almira horsemanship. Since the day he'd come to the Hamiltons, he had discreetly watched her at every turn, trying not to attract attention as he did so. Now, close observation of his student was legitimate and required. Daniel drank in her posture, the way she sat on her horse, grasped the reins with her gloved hands, the tilt of her head, her smile, and the melody of her voice. His good fortune in being able to have her all to himself, without interference or distraction, was a joy.

"Daniel," she asked. "Where do you come from? Please tell me about your life before you came to us."

Her interest was flattering, but Daniel didn't answer immediately. If Almira knew the truth, the whole truth about his childhood—the poverty, the wasting consumption and the drunken arguments—she would be disgusted.

"No one's ever asked me that before," he finally said. "But to start with, I don't come from a nice family like yours. Families like mine are common as dirt in Ireland. There's not much else to know." Daniel hoped this would satisfy her curiosity, but it didn't.

"And how did the Dwyers come to America?"

27

He let her question stand until he decided it best to answer. "My dad was a soldier for the king. He was with the lancers, and I learned about horses from him. He got a farm in Canada, but he lost it to drink. It ruined him, and my mum too. That's why I took the oath of temperance."

"You have? That is so noble."

Despite what she said, he didn't feel noble at all. "I've seen a lot of trouble made for people by gin and rum. The same could happen to me. Anyway, they both died in 1832. I've been on my own since then."

"How old were you?"

"When they passed? Eleven—maybe twelve. I worked for a livery in Halifax until the panic closed it down. After that, I worked my way here to the States."

"It sounds like an adventure," said Almira.

"An adventure?" Daniel laughed. "Bless me, no, I wouldn't call it that. Those were some hard years. Fortunately, I met your father and he hired me. I don't know if you realize how indebted I am to him and your mother. Your mum and dad have given me the only real home I've ever had. Your parents and you, and old Sandborne too."

The French tutor, Mr. Descharmes, was gone. Almira entered her mother's bedroom. Gloriana had been unwell for the last several days. Climbing stairs or even dressing were too much of an exertion, so she stayed abed. Her daughter took a seat at the window beside her, having brought her sewing basket and embroidery sampler with her.

"Are your French lessons progressing well, my dear?" Gloriana asked.

"*Oui*, Momma," Almira said. "It's such a graceful language."

They sat together. As her daughter worked, Gloriana offered praise, criticism, or instruction on the art of embroidery.

When she noticed Almira trying to conceal a mistake, Gloriana spoke up at once. "Remember Dolly," she said, trying to resist breaking into another fit of coughing, "the true object of embroidery is that it teaches a girl to master her impulses."

"But Momma, it's frustrating to rework something because of the slightest imperfection, especially when it's on the back."

Gloriana nodded. "No doubt it is, but such is life. You will find that even a hidden mistake left uncorrected can spoil all the best efforts which follow it."

Almira had almost finished with the alphabet in cross-stitch when her mother asked, "What do you two talk about whilst you ride?"

"You mean Daniel and me?"

"Yes."

"We talk of riding, of course, and other things," Almira said. "Daniel knows everything about horses. Did you know that his father was a British lancer?"

"I did not. And what else has he told you?"

"Oh, this and that," Almira said with nonchalance. "He did tell me he has taken an oath of temperance."

"Has he now?" Gloriana remarked with some interest. "That is commendable."

"I thought so too."

Almira worked on her sampler for a few minutes more. "Mama. When you met father, what was he like?"

Gloriana picked up a small china cup, stirred it with a tiny silver spoon, and took a careful sip. "He was then as he is now—very fixed in his ideas. Friends warned me he was stubborn and would grow disagreeable as he aged."

The constant wheezing in her lungs forced Gloriana to wait to catch her breath. "When he sets his mind to something, he will not be dissuaded until it is accomplished. He was so then and is that way still."

Almira pressed her with another question. "But did you think him handsome? How did you know you loved him?"

"I did think him handsome, yes," her mother said, smiling to herself at the memory of their first intimate experience. She took another sip of tea and swallowed. "But I will say it was not so much that I was in love with him, as that I knew he was dedicated to me."

Gloriana could see her daughter was a bit disappointed by the answer. Sensing Almira's need for explanation, she told her, "You see, I knew he would always provide for me and any children we should have together. It is natural to grow to love someone who devotes himself to you as your father has to me. That is the nature of enduring love."

Almira set down her sampler and sat on the bed beside her mother. "And what of Grandmother and Grandfather?" she asked, eyes cast downward. "Did they approve that he courted you?"

"They did not. Not until we'd been married for a long while. They eventually changed their minds."

"Why ever would they have objected?"

"There were several reasons but let us just say it was principally because I was so young."

Gloriana held up one finger to secure Almira's attention. She took a few shallow breaths and went on. "You must realize that the van Elsts had lost their fortune in the late war with the British. We were not impoverished but had fallen on hard times. After some few years had passed, my parents came to see your father as having restored me to the affluence I was born to through his own ambition—which of course he did, and more."

"Then Father was not a man of means when you met him?"

Intuiting her daughter's thoughts, Gloriana said lovingly. "Dolly, look at me. This is a delicate matter, but one that you and I ought to address." She collected her thoughts. "You are but a young lady, and the passions of youth are strong within you. While I am gladdened by the pleasure you take in your riding lessons, there are dangers in allowing your heart to be unbridled, just as an unbridled horse can lead its rider astray."

Almira kept her eyes cast down. Gloriana reached for her hand.

"But, Momma," Almira said in a faint voice, "what shall I do if my heart has already led me astray?"

"Then you must rein it in, my dear. It will hurt. Every association we have with others has its limitations, and no good can come if we ignore them. Enjoy your friendship with Daniel for what it is and not for what it can never be, however much you might wish it otherwise."

Almira leaned forward and fell on her mother's bosom, not in tears, but heartbroken nevertheless.

Gloriana petted her girl's hair and her shoulders.

"Ah, Mirie," she soothed. "Because you are my only living child and on the brink of womanhood, I will tell you something that will be confidential. Between us, I know all these things from my own experience. Trust me. The pain of denying yourself is far less than the pain that follows the pleasure of indulgence."

Chapter 7

October, 1970

In the morning David woke early and cooked up pastrami and eggs. The night before had been cold, so the aroma of cooking and coffee gave their breakfast a cozy feeling. He told Angela he wanted to show her the carriage house and the way he intended to set it up as an antique shop.

As they walked across the yard toward the building, he explained, "I'm going to paint a sign with 'Carriage House Antiques' in big old-fashioned, serifed letters, so people can see it from the road."

Opening the doors, David pointed to where he intended to put display cases and another area he thought would be perfect for refinishing furniture. "This place is in really good shape." He stepped to one corner and ran his hands over a table fitted out with shelves and a stationary vice. "Like this old workbench."

David continued the tour. "That ladder over there goes up to a loft crammed-full of cool old stuff. I've been up there once or twice to poke around and it's full to the rafters. In another month or so I'm going to start emptying it out. God only knows what I'll find."

"It's a big treasure hunt for you," said Angela. "Isn't it?"

"You're right. It is." He leaned against the Ghia, folded his arms, and surveyed the roughhewn rafters. "It's like buying out an abandoned storage locker. The same kind of excitement in not knowing what's inside. Except this place is on a massive scale and much older. I doubt anyone has lived here since World War One."

Angela reached for the tarpaulin. "Hey, when are we going to go for a ride? Let's go this afternoon."

"Sure," David agreed. "We can run up to Plattsburgh. There's supposed to be a Chinese place up there. We'll take the Northway and be there in forty-five minutes, maybe an hour."

"Really, is that all?"

"Don't be sarcastic. It's a beautiful drive, especially at this time of year."

They wandered over to the barn. It was dirtier and a lot rougher. He pointed to the massive, wooden beams. "There isn't a nail in this whole place," David said, proud as a new father. "The whole thing is pegged together. Can you believe it?"

While admiring the building, David spotted something behind a broken-down tractor. It was covered with engine parts and a half-case of motor oil, but there it was. The Grecian divan he'd seen the spirit sitting on night after night, the one she sat upon when he spoke to her. "Hey," he said to Angela as he started to clear off the debris. "Help me get this out, would you?"

She looked at him with suspicion. "You really want this thing? It's filthy."

"Yes. This is a good piece of antique furniture."

She stepped toward it but stopped. "How do I know there aren't mice in it?"

"You don't."

Angela made a face. She wasn't going to come any closer, but David knew his girl was incapable of backing down from a challenge. "You're not scared, are you?"

It worked.

Once they had the daybed out in the open, he could see it much better. The piece was of a single roll-armed style, classically inspired, early nineteenth century. Typical of what was fashionable from 1800 to about 1850. It had been upholstered in red velvet, but that was a long time ago. Now it was faded, sagging, chewed open by rodents, draped in spider webs and bird droppings. The ornately carved wood frame, however, was intact and solid. But even more exciting, it was the very same piece of furniture the so-called Miss Hamilton sat upon when she appeared. Here, in three dimensions, sat a tangible, fully material item that seemed to corroborate his otherworldly experience. For some reason though, David kept this from Angela. He didn't want to try explaining Almira to her or anyone else.

"Angela," he said. "This is a really early piece."

"What's it worth?" she asked.

"As it is now, not much. Even completely reupholstered, this Empire stuff doesn't get a lot of attention, but I like it. I have a hunch it was part of the original furnishings in the house."

The sound of a truck came up the driveway. The battered, older Chevy ground to a stop outside. A barrel-chested, middle aged man got out.

"Hi there," said David.

The man waved, stepped closer, and offered his hand. There was a faint scent of manure about him. "I'm Gary LeBerge. My dairy is the next place up the road. You just buy this old house?"

"Yeah, I did," David said. "I'm Dave Weis, and this is my girlfriend, Angela."

There was another round of handshaking. LeBerge's hands were rough and incredibly large. "I'm going to go wash up," said Angela. "It was nice to meet you, Mr. LeBerge."

As she walked off, the farmer commented, "That's a real pretty girl you got there." He shook his head, as if to clear his thoughts. "So, you gonna live in the house, or are you going to knock it down?"

"Live in it—at least part of it—until I get it all fixed up."

LeBerge whistled. "You've got your work cut out for you."

"That's all right," David said. "I like old buildings."

"Boy, I hope so, 'cause there's a lot of history in this old place."

The man's words piqued David's curiosity. "Like what?"

"I dunno. Stories. Some people around here say it's a haunted house. My uncle always said so, but you know how people talk."

David wanted details, so he tried again. "Like what? What have you heard?"

"Well, my uncle, Loyal, he used to caretake this place back when he was a kid in the '30s. There was a lot of problems around here with hoboes during the Depression. Anyhow, he told me that for a while he tried sleeping downstairs, but he kept waking up in the middle of the night. He'd hear someone crying, people arguing—weird shit like that.

He said that one night he heard noises upstairs, right? So he goes up there to see what's going on."

"And what happened?" said David with impatience.

"Uncle Loyal swore there was the sound of somebody crying coming from this one room upstairs, and when he opened the door there was a girl sitting there just crying her face off."

"That's creepy," David said.

"Damn straight it's creepy. He told me he slept in his car from that night on. I've seen some weird shit around this place too."

"Like what?"

"Weird lights. You know, when the leaves are all down, I can see this place from my house pretty clear. A few times I swore I could see lights on. Not bright lights but, you know, like some glowing lights. I'd drive over to check it out, and when I'd get here, they'd be gone. Then I'd drive home, and I'd see them again."

LeBerge's head cranked around, scanning the house and property. "So, you tell me. I believe in ghosts. The wife says there's no such a-thing, but I believe it, anyhow." He pulled off his tractor cap and wiped his forehead. "So, what do you do for work?"

That was an awkward question for David. He'd have to answer it on the fly. "I used to have a psychotherapy practice in the city," he said. "I've gotten out of that, now. Actually, I intend to set up the carriage house as an antique shop. I thought I'd get that rolling this year, but you know how that goes."

"Oh shit, yeah. My wife has a motto. 'Everything takes longer, and costs more than you plan for.' And one other thing; 'it's always later than you think.'"

With the way things were going—repairs, parts, man-hours of labor—David had to agree.

"Anyway, if you don't have someone lined up to plow this driveway in the winter, I can do it for you. Thirty bucks a month, no matter how often I need to come out. I'll just come on over anytime we get more than four or five inches. I'm up at three in the morning anyway, so you'll always be able to get out."

David took a spiral notepad from his shirt pocket and wrote down his neighbor's number. "Let's take care of November right now." He handed over a few bills from his wallet.

"Roger that. If we get an early snow this month, it's on me. Anyway, the wife says I better get something done today, but it's been good to meet you."

LeBerge drove away. David returned his attention to the daybed, resolving to find someone he could trust to re-upholster it. Then he'd restore it to its proper place in the Quiet Room. Doing so would please Miss Hamilton.

Back inside the house, Angela was in the bathroom applying lipstick.

"Hey," she said as he came into the kitchen. "That guy was a hoot."

"He liked you," David said.

"Oh really? Well, I liked his cologne."

She came out in a short red dress, make-up with false eyelashes, fish-net stockings, and platforms.

"Alright doctor, I'm ready for our big night out on the town in— what was it? Plattville?"

"Plattsburgh," David corrected.

"Plattsburgh, right."

She looked great, he thought, even if overdressed in a New York City kind of way.

"So, don't we have to make reservations?"

He doubted it. "Tell you what," he said anyway. "The phone book is on the counter. You check and see if there's even a Chinese place there. In the meantime, I'll go get the car ready. I haven't taken it out on the road since I got the truck."

Back in the carriage house, David walked himself through the well-practiced ritual: unzip the cover, fold it carefully and put it away. Check the oil. Re-attach the battery cables. Try the ignition. The engine turned over immediately and purred like a kitten. He let her warm-up. "Man, I love this car," he said to himself.

His thoughts turned to Angela. Her naivety about life in the "North Country" was cute, kind of sexy, really. As he stepped through the kitchen door, she was hanging up the phone.

"You won't believe this," Angela said. "The only place is called AAA Chinese. And, no, we don't need a reservation."

"Do they clean your windshield too?" Joked David.

She laughed hard. "I can't believe we're gonna eat at a place called AAA Chinese."

35

"I know. It sounds swanky. I'll go put on a clean shirt and tie."

Angela followed him into the next room.

"You know…" She wrapped her arms around his waist and brushed her face across his shoulder blades. "Since there's no reservation, maybe we don't have to leave right away. Maybe we can waste a little time first."

The trip was great. Angela tucked her hair inside a beret, and they drove with the top down. The ride had a holiday atmosphere. Getting off the highway at the main Plattsburgh exit, they stopped at the first phone booth they saw, called and got directions to a strip-mall near the Air Force base. As they walked in it was obvious that AAA Chinese was strictly a take-out joint.

"What do you think," Angela whispered in his ear as they read the menu on the wall above the counter. "Are we overdressed?"

"Not if we go up to Montreal, no."

"Are you for real?"

"Sure," said David. "Why not? It's not that far, and there's supposed to be some great discotheques up there. Let's eat and run on up."

For David, a romantic meal in the car wasn't so bad. With the top up, the feeling was whimsically intimate. After the fortune cookies were read.

"Wash hands in morning and neck at night," for her.

"The object of your desire comes closer," for him.

They threw the paper plates, cardboard containers and plastic utensils in the parking lot trash can. By the time they were on the freeway outside Plattsburgh it was getting dark. Angela lit a cigarette and looked around.

"Christ," she said. "There's nothing—no lights or anything. Where did everybody go?"

"Mostly they moved away."

"What happened?"

"This part of the country never recovered from the Civil War. All the commercial traffic on the lake and canals ended, and those who weren't killed in the war moved west."

Another hour's drive brought them to Montreal, a place where everyone spoke French, and no one would admit to speaking English.

They danced at a club with loud music, strobe lights, and go-go dancers in elevated cages. It seemed sophisticated and cosmopolitan—on par with any discotheque they'd been to in New York City, but with a decidedly European flavor.

It was after three in the morning when they finally started home. David drove. Sometime after re-crossing the border, Angela rested her head on his shoulder. He had to clear his mind for this stretch of deserted highway, with the drone of the engine surrounding them, was a good place for it.

Since the visitations in the quiet room had started, everything felt so unsettled. Until now, he'd thought he had it all figured out. There was no God. There was only the material world which could be observed, measured, objectively quantified. It made sense. It was bleak, but it was tidy. Anyone who insisted on a religious belief, well, that was an infantile artifact, the need for an omnipotent mother figure. Psychology was clear on this point, but these apparitions were really upsetting the apple cart.

Angela's head grew even heavier.

She must be sound asleep, he thought. David looked back on the weekend. That thing she told him yesterday—that he couldn't believe in ghosts and not believe in God as well—was still on his mind. He had to admit her comments on his life were insightful, but almost always inconvenient.

Chapter 8

July, 1840

Fidgety with expectation, Almira waited while Daniel fetched the horses from the paddock and saddled them.

At his approach, Almira pronounced in mock formality, "Well, my gallant young lancer, where shall we ride today?"

"I would like to take you to my favorite spot," said Daniel. "That is, of course, if that suits you."

"That sounds so lovely. Is it far?"

"No, not far at all."

Almira stepped onto the mounting stone. It made her almost as tall as Daniel. She caught the scent of soap. He must have just shaved. Daniel held Ginger Snap by the bridle while Almira mounted. He got on Marcus and they set off toward the lake. The pair turned their horses northward as they'd done before, riding at an easy pace.

"Daniel," asked Almira. "Am I progressing well in my equestrian skills?"

"If you're asking whether you're better at riding horses, I'd say definitely. Just remember, Ginger Snap is a gentle horse. She wants to be ridden gently."

"And Bonnie, father's new horse?" asked Almira.

Daniel smiled. "Bonnie's a good carriage horse, I suppose, but she's a lot older than your father thinks. That's why he can drive her so easily with the buggy. Now, Marcus here is more spirited. He likes a good gallop. You see, Miss Almira, every horse is different. I think that's why I love horses."

Instead of turning from the lane as usual, the pair rode a hundred yards farther to a remote corner of Hamilton's land. Here they brought their horses to a stop. It was the crest of a small hillock overlooking the water, nearby to a small grove of trees.

Almira twisted in her sidesaddle and looked around. "This is your favorite spot. Am I right?"

"Yes, it is," said Daniel. "How did you know?"

"I know this place. I used to bring mother here when she was stronger. My brothers and sister are buried in the wood over there."

"Not in a churchyard?" Daniel sounded puzzled.

"No." Almira shook her head. "Mother said she could not bear her babies exposed to the beating sun or the cold of winter. My father has no belief, so they are buried together in a little cemetery of their own, protected by the trees."

"If you like, we can rest here," said Daniel.

"But Mr. Dwyer, there are no large stones here. Please help me down lest I stumble." She walked her horse forward a few more steps, searching for the right location.

"Of course, Miss Mirie." He dismounted and reached up toward her.

As she slipped from the saddle Almira felt Daniel place his hands firmly around her waist, his fingertips nearly touching. He lowered her to the ground, and they came face to face for a brief but wonderful instant. The pulsing surging through her body seemed about to burst the confines of her corset. Above them, clouds raced across the sky and below, all the greenery was fresh.

Steady on the ground, Almira removed her leghorn hat and let it dangle from her hand by the ribbons. A few yards away rose a slight rock ledge with a lawn of new clover behind it. It looked inviting, so she sat down by this lush carpet with her knees pulled up together. Daniel tethered the horses to a nearby tree and sat cross legged beside her.

"This is such a glorious view," she said. "I can see why this is your favorite place."

"Yes, it's peaceful," he said. "I come out here when I can. I sit and think about all sorts of things—imagine the whole world. Sometimes

I bring a newspaper and read."

They watched a steamboat pass, on its way to Whitehall. It was pulling four canal boats loaded with freight from Burlington.

"I read about a steamboat that caught fire and sank last winter," Almira said. "Those poor people all drowned."

"That was the *Lexington*," said Daniel. "It sank in the Long Island Sound last January."

Almira shuddered and leaned closer, placing a hand on Daniel's arm. "It would be so dreadful to drown in that frigid water."

When he turned her face was only inches from his. His kiss became the only thought she could entertain, but Daniel turned his attention back to the lake. "It would be horrible," he stammered. "I can hardly imagine it."

"Look." Almira pointed. "There comes a large sailing ship."

"She is a large ship, yes." As the vessel approached, Daniel said, "Do you see she has two masts? That's a schooner. In fact, I think she's the *General Scott*, a new ship built just last year." He went on explaining the differences between a skiff and a schooner, but Almira interrupted him.

"This is so lovely." She fell backwards into the clover, sprawled with her back arched and cheeks flushed with excitement. She drew her hands near her face, feeling her fingernails pressing into her palms.

Daniel turned toward her. "Miss Mirie, we've known each other a long time, haven't we?"

"Since we were but youngsters." She studied Daniel's every feature, cleft chin and blue eyes, searching for a sign he had any idea how thoroughly she was in love with him.

"Well," he said. "I've been thinking. While the weather is good, maybe we ought to have as many riding lessons as we can."

Nearly breathless, her heart pounding, she could say nothing. The silence between them stretched on, her looking up at him, him down at her.

Finally, Daniel swallowed hard and said, "Miss Almira, can I ask you a question?"

"*Gardez la coeur*," she whispered.

"What did you say?"

She parted her lips to speak but could find no voice. Almira quivered all over. Daniel leaned across her. They kissed, broke apart, looked into each other's eyes and kissed again.

The summer unfolded into the happiest Almira could remember. She organized her life around arranging her next sidesaddle instruction, for she'd grown to love being held, caressed, and feeling him pressed against her body. She ached for it. Whenever Mr. Hamilton left for any extended period, she would rush to her mother's side for permission to go riding. Sometimes it was granted with the usual precautions, at other times, and more frequently as the season progressed, Gloriana Hamilton was too ill or too sedated with laudanum to respond.

In either case, Almira ran into her drawing room to quickly adjust her hair, pinch her cheeks, and bite her lips to redden them, then don her velvet riding habit and rush to the mounting stone.

Daniel was usually already waiting. They rode to the promontory by the copse of trees, dismount and let the horses graze. Out of sight, the lovers talked in tender voices punctuated by sweet kisses.

One afternoon, as they sat together at the rock ledge, Daniel ran his fingers through the clover behind them.

"What are you doing?" Almira asked.

"I'm looking for a clover with four leaves. For good luck's sake."

"But Danny," she said, chiding him. "Isn't that make-believe? There aren't really such things."

"Yes, there are, and I'll keep looking till I find one. Someday I will—you'll see." He continued to hunt absently until he looked up. "Sometimes I wonder what other places are like," he said. "You know, a lot of people have gone off to Wisconsin and Michigan. I think about what it's like there in those places. Do you ever wonder about things like that?"

"I do. Great cities, the sea. We both want to see something of the world, don't we?"

Daniel had an idea. "You've seen all the books above your father's desk? Do you think he'd let me read any of them? I think about the things I might do if I had more education."

Almira closed her eyes and offered her lips again. Daniel kissed her hungrily. When she let them flutter open again, Sandborne was rounding the trees not a dozen yards away.

"Oh no." She shrieked and broke away, covering her face behind her hands.

The old man looked up from his sheep, surprised to find himself face to face with the couple, still in each other's arms. Daniel whirled around. Sandborne brought his hand to the brim of his hat and backed away.

"Come along now ladies, there's nothing for us to see here." He told the half dozen sheep with him.

The next morning brought a warm, humid day, with the rumble of distant thunder warning of rainstorms. Seeing Sandborne enter the carriage house from the window of her sitting room, Almira hurried down the back staircase and across the yard.

The side door of the carriage house stood ajar. She stepped in quietly. Inside, it smelled of manly things: leather, lumber, tobacco. Sandborne stood at the workbench, stitching a piece of harness clamped in a vice. She knocked on the door jamb. "Mr. Sandborne," she ventured.

"Aye, miss," he said, with a nod.

Closing the door behind her, Almira approached him. "May I have a confidential word with you?"

"What can I do for you, miss?"

Almira dreaded raising the subject of the day before but knew it couldn't be ignored. Finally, with hesitation, she spoke. "Mr. Sandborne, I fear that you may have gotten the wrong impression when you came upon Daniel and me yesterday. I assure you—it is not as it may appear. To avoid troubling my father unnecessarily, I beg you not—"

Sandborne held up his calloused hand. "Miss, you needn't say anything more to me. I saw nothing but a flock of sheep. Your secret is safe with Sandborne."

Just the sound of the words your secret made Almira blush with embarrassment, but a flood of relief and gratitude followed the emotion. "God bless you, sir. I am in your debt, but I beg you not to think ill of me. I should be mortified if that were the case."

"It may surprise you, miss, but I was also young once," he said to her. "Young and in love."

"Mr. Sandborne, I never thought of you as—"

"Young? Why would you, miss? It is a long time since, and now I am grown old."

Sandborne, young and in love? The very thought was hard to imagine. Almira's curiosity forced her to ask, "And, where is she? What happened?"

"She was taken away. I rarely think of her anymore."

Large droplets of rain, at first like individual tears, then in driving sheets, fell on the building and window over the workbench. A loud clap of thunder cracked. Looking at Sandborne, with his whisker stubble and weathered features, she could see sadness in him for the first time.

"There's too much sorrow in this world and the joys are few. No, I'll not spoil young people's happiness while they can find it, so don't worry. But please be very careful," he cautioned. "Your father would not understand."

Chapter 9

December 3rd, 1970

The contents of the carriage house needed to be inventoried before freezing temperatures made the job impossible. David started by emptying out the loft. Accessible by way of a steep stair—more of a ladder—he poked his head through the hatch. The silence was palpable, as if he were disturbing a crypt which had been sealed for centuries.

Upper lofts of carriage houses were commonly used as living quarters for farm hands. David knew this, but it was clear no one had lived up here in decades.

Wading through the stacks of miscellany packed in the loft was a difficult job. Since it would have been impossible to bring anything larger than a trundle bed into the loft, what was stored there seemed like one solid mass of cartons, boxes, and portable items under an even layer of dust. When anything was touched or moved, clouds of it floated up and caused him to sneeze.

In truth, most of these things were, if once valuable, now worthless—crumbling newspapers, cracked pieces of crockery. There were some nice very collectable antique tools. A hand drill, gramophone, and a set of early kitchen chairs were brought down the ladder and set off to one side.

Back in the loft, with room to maneuver, David took a few minutes to let the dust settle and survey what remained. In one corner, behind a few crates of old tack, stood a stack of framed pictures. He brushed away cobwebs, sneezed twice and pulled them out. The frame edges

45

closest to the small gable window had a build-up of bird droppings. In front was a portrait of General William Henry Harrison, next a pair of early prints titled in turn, "Which Will I Marry?" and "Isabelle."

Peering into a cranny, he saw one more. David reached into the shadows and brought out a large memorial. Watercolor tinted, it depicted all the clichés of early nineteenth-century mourning. Two weeping willows, a lamb resting beneath one of them, and a woman in a black dress with fashionable balloon sleeves, sobbing into a handkerchief and leaning over a monument on which had been handwritten.

In loving memory of Almira van Elst Hamilton.
Born November 16th, 1822
Died December 21st, 1841
Gone but not forgotten.

David froze. His pulse quickened with the realization that this had to be her, the woman he dreamt of or imagined or with whom he actually had conversations—he still wasn't entirely sure which.

His heart pounded, and in his haste to clean and examine the memorial closely, David was already on his way down the ladder when another thought stopped him short. What if something else was tucked away in that corner under the eaves? He scrambled back into the loft. Reaching blindly with his outstretched hand, he felt only rough-hewn lumber, part of the carriage house roof. He was about to give up when his fingertips grazed short, coarse fur. David pulled back his hand, frightened it could be a woodchuck or raccoon, but there was no sound or movement. He tried again. Yes, coarse fur, but also rows of tacks and blunt corners. Stretched out on his belly, he was able to grasp whatever it was and pull it out.

A small trunk about thirty inches long with cowhide covered wood shaped like a loaf of bread came out. It had heavy leather handles on each end and substantial brass tacks placed along all the edges. The same tacks formed the initials AVH on the lid.

With both treasures in the kitchen under brighter lighting, David got to work. The memorial cleaned up easily with vinegar and paper towels. Propping it on the countertop, he looked it over, admiring its artificial wood-grained frame and the innocent symbolism it displayed.

This memorial was for the girl in the Quiet Room. David knew at once he would hang it above his desk.

He turned his attention to the trunk. This would take more effort. David brushed and vacuumed the hide cover, repeating the process twice more. Applying a generous amount of neatsfoot oil and then Vaseline on the dry and hard leather handles helped some of their old luster to emerge.

The brass lock was still secured. As far as he could tell, it had been for well over a century. Of course there was no key, but in the bathroom he found a few of Angela's bobby pins on the back of the sink. He took one, straightened it, and jimmied it around inside the lock. At first it didn't work, but after squirting oil in the mechanism he tried again. It popped.

David took a deep breath, his heart beating with suspense. Raising the lid, he found a collection of items once neatly stowed, folded and stacked, though now, unsettled. Unpacking it had to be done methodically, like an archaeological dig.

On the top lay a small branch. Judging by the fragments of dried organic matter littering the inside of the trunk and the thorns on the stem, he guessed it was from a rose bush. What sentimental impulse had driven someone to save it, he wondered. He set it aside.

Next, he lifted out two hair combs—one quite large, of horn, and the other, smaller and more detailed, of German silver. After that, came a folded textile made of black silk. David lifted it carefully and found he held up an apron. Its wide waistband fastened with three tiny, flat, brass wire hooks and eyes. The borders and waistband were finely embroidered with flowers in silk floss, still bright and vibrant. A few he recognized—pansies, daisies, tulips.

Several books were in the trunk. One was large, though not very thick. *Mossrose Album* was embossed on the cover. Opening it, he saw that it was an autograph book filled with trite sentiments and poems, all inscribed in variations of tiny, feminine handwriting. A souvenir, of some sort.

Last, was a larger volume of a few hundred pages. *The Young Lady's Friend* was lettered on the spine. Wasn't this the very book Miss Hamilton was reading the night she first appeared? He opened it and smelled old paper. On the flyleaf was written, "Beloved daughter, our

Lord calls me back to his side where I shall soon be reunited with your sister and brothers. Though I must leave, let this book guide you in my absence. Allow the words to be my voice as you grow into womanhood. Your loving Mother, Gloriana van Elst Hamilton."

David's mind reeled. Either he accepted the possibility, no, probability of spirit visitation or he was unaware of his own hallucinations. He'd have to be in severe psychosis for that, but no one had questioned his state of mind or grasp of reality. There were no recent arrests or hospitalizations, either. Incredibly, the David-is-losing-his-mind theory was the less plausible of the two.

He set the book aside. At the bottom of the trunk lay a handkerchief with something hard wrapped inside. Unfolding the silk, a small leatherette case was revealed. David recognized it as the type used for early photographs.

He released the brass catches that held it closed. It opened like a book to reveal the daguerreotype of a young woman. Having spent its lifetime in a dark and protected casket, her image was breathtaking in its depth and clarity. He'd seen daguerreotypes like this before, but only a few.

In silver tones with hints of color, surrounded by an octagonal, stippled brass matte, the image depicted a female figure caught on the cusp between girl and womanhood, staring coyly from within her bonnet. He recognized the face immediately—Miss Almira Hamilton.

She wore clothes apropos of a summer's day; a short-sleeved dress with a white lace pelisse pinned in front. It hung from her bare shoulders to her elbows.

In the Quiet Room, it was impossible to look directly into Almira's eyes. The way they darted around or remained fixed on her sewing prevented eye contact for more than the most fleeting moment. Now he could study her eyes carefully and did so for several minutes. They gave the impression of polite unease. David noticed the constricted pupils. She must have been sitting in full sunlight.

Almira's features were feminine and perfectly symmetrical. His eyes traced the course of her neck. Her chin. The curve of her slightly parted lips. It would be so easy to fall in love with a girl like this.

Chapter 10

October 12th, 1840

George Hamilton had already been gone two days, negotiating with business partners in Plattsburgh for the construction of a new ship to carry freight the length of Lake Champlain. Daniel and Almira tried to take advantage of the opportunity to find time together, but the necessity of work on the property and persistent, drizzling rain prevented riding lessons. Despite all this, daylight revealed a bright, crisp autumn world, the mountains streaked yellow and orange.

Almira was picking apples in the orchard when Daniel ambled up to her.

"Good morning, sweet," he said in a low voice.

"And to you too, sir. I hoped you would see me out here."

He stepped close enough for their fingertips to mingle, but no more; even at this distance they had to be careful.

"If I work quickly, I think I can be free for an hour or two later this afternoon. We can go riding."

Almira's heart flooded with anticipation. She ached to be kissed, kissed by *him*, even while standing in the brisk October morning with a basket of apples on her arm. The need was overwhelming. But even stealing the quickest kiss was too dangerous. She did not dare.

"Watch for me from your window around three o'clock."

"I will," she said, wiggling her fingers discreetly under her chin.

When the basket was full of low-hanging fruit, Almira brought it inside the kitchen. Julia stood at the window, ironing linens, setting aside those items that needed mending.

"Julia, has my mother been up today?"

"No, miss. When I brought Mrs. Hamilton her pitcher and towel, she was still asleep."

Almira took one of the apples from the basket, cut out the core and sliced it into small sections, eating one as she did so. Hopefully, mother wouldn't ask much of her today. Maybe she would take her nostrum and sleep without asking to be read to or ask Almira to pat her back as one might burp a baby. Almira knew these thoughts were selfish, but the anticipation of being alone with Daniel pushed all other considerations aside.

"Julia," she said. "Please prepare a tray with sliced apples and tea for my mother and bring it to her."

Hurrying upstairs, she found her mother in bed, propped up on one elbow, coughing into a blood sprinkled handkerchief. She raised desperate eyes but was unable to draw enough breath to speak.

"Mama, drink some water," Almira urged. She held up a glass for her to sip from, the way she had so many times in recent years. As she did so, she couldn't help but notice how much her mother had aged, even in the last few weeks. Her hair was now nearly as gray as it was brown, and she'd lost an alarming amount of weight. Her skin sagged from her face and neck.

"Thank you, Dolly," she finally said in a hoarse voice. "That is better."

Julia came into the room and placed a tray on a table nearby. "Will there be anything else, Miss?"

"No, Julia, that will be all," Almira said. She rose and brought the tray over to the bed. "Here's a nice cup of tea for you and some apple slices. I picked them myself just this morning."

Gloriana reached for the cup and drank from it. She smiled weakly. "Ah, good. Cream and sugar." She handed the cup back and shifted how she lay. "Mirie, darling, please help me sit up."

Once arranged, Almira sat on the bed with her mother, watching her sipped the tea and nibbled the apple slices.

"What have you to do today?" she asked her daughter between persistent coughs.

"I have a French lesson to translate for Mr. Descharmes," Almira said. "And since the weather is so pretty, I was hoping I could receive a riding lesson later this afternoon."

Laboring to swallow some tea, her mother didn't answer immediately. Almira took the opportunity to embellish her story with a harmless fabrication.

"Ginger Snap is such a spirited horse. Daniel says that only by frequently riding her will she acquire better habits."

Gloriana Hamilton looked out the window to the beautiful October day. "Very well, then," she said. "I feel very tired today. I have to rest, but do see me before you go riding. I have something important I want to tell you."

While translating at her writing table, Almira looked up again at the clock on the wall. It was not quite three. A fly bumbled against the window, and Wigwam chased it across the glass panes. With little choice but to wait, she forced herself to go back to her French assignment.

Finally, Daniel emerged from the paddock, leading Marcus and Ginger Snap by the reins. Almira raised the window sash and waved her hand in the air. "I'll be there in a moment," she called. She slammed her book closed, capped her inkwell, and blotted her pen nib."

I should check on Mother.

Trying to be quiet, Almira crept down the hallway to Gloriana's room and peeked inside. Relieved to see her mother sleeping, she turned to leave when Gloriana spoke.

"Dolly, is that you?" she said, straining to be heard.

All the more frustrated at having been addressed by her pet name, Almira rolled her eyes.

"Yes, Momma. Is there something you need?"

"I heard you call out to someone."

"Yes, that was Daniel. He waits for me with the horses."

"Dolly," Gloriana whispered. "Please sit here with me for just a minute. Hold my hand."

"But Mother, Daniel is waiting."

"Please," her mother implored.

The awkward silenced stretched between them, Almira unwilling to come closer and Gloriana unwilling to release her. Finally, Gloriana spoke. "I understand, but please come see me when you return."

"Thank you, Momma. I won't be long," she said and left.

In her room, Almira quickly brushed her hair and dampened her face with a lavender towel. She pulled on her velvet riding habit, laced on her leather shoes and tied her plaid bonnet ribbons in a coquettish bow under her chin. Wigwam watched it all with feline detachment. "You're in charge until I return," she told him.

That afternoon, Daniel and Almira rode along the lake until well out of sight. They dismounted and walked hand in hand to the familiar copse of trees along the rock ledge where they sat together. Clouds flew overhead and beyond the mountains, throwing shadows on the lake and landscape as they advanced across the sky.

"Danny," she said, snuggling closer, "Father mentioned that you borrowed a book from him last week. What was it?"

"Lyell's *Principles of Geology*. He gave me some old newspapers too. It was very kind of him."

"Is it interesting?" she asked.

"The book? I suppose it is, yes," he said. "But what was more interesting to me was an article in one of the newspapers about the daguerreotype."

"Dag, dagero—"

"Daguerreotype, I think. I'm not entirely sure. However, it's pronounced, the daguerreotype is a method to capture a person's likeness on a silver plate. Imagine if your reflection on a looking glass could be frozen in place, in miniature as some people say. I think it is like that."

"I can't imagine it."

"I'll bring that newspaper with me next time. We can read it together."

"Good, you can teach me all about this dag—"

"Daguerreotype."

"Right, daguerreotype," she repeated again, carefully. "We'll need to find some new lessons for me when winter comes." She said it jokingly, but the subject was a serious one. Finding an hour or two when and where they had reason to be together, let alone unchaperoned, would be hard to do in winter, no matter how careful they were. Footprints left in the snow tell tales.

"Maybe when I've read all of your father's books it can be different," said Daniel as they rode back. "But he doesn't think I'm educated enough for you now, I know it."

"Father feels no such way," Almira countered. It was a lie, but why think about this problem now. "It'll take time for him to get used to us, but I'll persuade him slowly, and he'll come around, you'll see."

As they rode into the yard by the carriage house, Sandborne strode up briskly. "Daniel, see to it that the horses are put away at once."

It was unlike Sandborne to be so abrupt. Daniel had a mystified look on his face, but the old man offered no explanations. "Please, son, just do as I'm telling you," Sandborne insisted. He turned to Almira. "Miss, please come with me."

She dismounted. "Mr. Sandborne, whatever is wrong?"

"Miss Almira, I have sad news. It's your mother. She's gone."

Almira wondered where her mother could have possibly gone to... Sandborne's meaning struck her. "No, that can't be," she cried. "I just spoke to her this afternoon." He tried to reach for her, but she broke away and ran toward the house, up the front steps where Julia sat, looking shaken.

"Mother, Mother," Almira called out as she burst through the door and up the stairway. At the bedroom entrance she stopped. Gloriana Hamilton lay there, half upright on the bolster, just as she'd left her a few hours earlier. She must be sleeping, Almira thought, the laudanum makes her sleep so deeply.

Almira stepped toward the bed.

"Mother, it's me, Mirie. Are you awake?"

There was no response. She sat on the bed and took her mother's hand. It was cold and without a will of its own—that of a corpse. She brought the hand to her face and pressed it to her cheek.

"Oh Momma," Almira said, through a rising storm of tears. "I didn't know. I'm so, so sorry." She threw herself down, crying into her mother's fragile, lifeless shoulder.

"Momma, please, please say something."

Sandborne walked into the room, followed by Daniel and Julia. He placed a hand on her shoulder.

"It's too late, child. She's gone."

Almira turned to them. "What happened?" she said. "Julia, tell me what happened."

"I don't know, miss. When I came in to fetch her piddle-pot, she was already gone."

"You mean she died alone? All alone, with no one here?"

Almira stood and stepped forward. Julia backed out of the room. "I didn't know, miss. It's not my fault."

Almira looked at Daniel, his eyes red. She looked at her mother. Her head hung at a horrifying angle.

"Please, miss, she's right," Sandborne said. "It's not the girl's fault. It's nobody's fault."

Almira woke up bewildered. What time was it? Why was she lying abed? Hamilton walked in, and as he did, she remembered what had taken place.

"Father," she asked. "Is it true? Is Momma really gone?"

He sat on the bed beside her, his face weary and swollen from grief. "Yes, it is so."

Hamilton stroked his daughter's hair. "You fainted. I was concerned for you, but you are awake now." He held her hand. "The Reverend Shedd is here, and some of our friends from Wilsborough."

Almira looked away, facing the wall.

"Come," her father said, "Come give mother your final regards."

The thought filled Almira with terror. On her last chance to speak with her mother, she'd done all she could to avoid her. This time, no matter how much she dreaded it, Almira knew facing her mother was impossible to avoid. Hamilton held out his arm for support, and they walked dreamlike down the hallway to Gloriana's bedroom.

Inside, several lamps and candles were lit. Some women from church had already prepared the body and dressed it in a shroud.

The Reverend Shedd stood to one side, reciting scripture.

With hands folded across her chest, Gloriana appeared surreal. Two churchwomen with whom Almira was barely acquainted approached her.

"She is at rest now," said one.

The other added, "Her suffering has ended, you must rejoice in her triumph."

If only these people knew how she had deserted her mother for an hour's secret pleasure, Almira thought, they wouldn't treat her so kindly. Someone placed a small scissor in her hand.

"You will wish to have a lock of your mother's hair," they said.

Shaking, Almira needed her father to hold her wrist to steady it. In fact, her hand had to be pulled toward her mother's head. Hamilton held a twisted tendril, ready to be harvested.

In the dim candlelight, with all these unfamiliar people crowded around her, Almira wished to bolt, the way she always feared Ginger Snap would someday do. Mr. Weldin asked if she would like fingernail clippings.

She declined with a quick shake of her head and instead, longing for a last chance to be with her mother, Almira knelt on the floor beside the bed. She reached for one of her mother's hands. It was cold, lifeless, and, already growing stiff, seemed to resist Almira's effort to bring it to her face.

After a short while Hamilton lifted his daughter to her feet. "Come, Almira," he whispered.

"Here child," said one of the ladies. "This is your mother's Bible, and this tract of mourning poetry is our gift to you. Your dear mother's lock is placed at a special poem."

"Thank you," she said softly to the woman. "Will you help me back? I must retire."

Almira thanked her at the door, relieved to be alone. The night had a feeling of unreality. She sat on the daybed, wondering what life would be like without her mother, someone whose life had been taken up with so much sadness and suffering. Why did she deserve this? To grieve for lost children and waste away year after year, and then die alone? Almira picked up the tract given her. She opened it and read the poem at which the lock of hair had been placed.

To MOTHERLESS DAUGHTERS
Remember what her voice hath said,
Who now in dust is laid,
And treasure every loving word,
Like flowers that cannot fade.
And let her counsels be your guide,
As you in stature grow,
Hers was that wisdom of the skies,
That draws the sting from woe.

The poem did not move her. Even the lock of hair between her fingers seemed vacant and lifeless. Almira picked up the Bible. She opened it to a random page and read, "Give thanks in all circumstances; for this is the will of God in Christ Jesus."

A tremendous anger rose and spilled over as boiling water might from a pot. All those horrid women. Drunk on death—and these sanctimonious recitations about its virtues—Almira could see none of it. Give thanks, indeed. Thanks for nothing. She wanted her mother alive, not triumphant in death. "Goddamn their lies." She hurled the Bible against the wall.

Chapter 11

December, 1970

As he came through the doorway, Almira looked up from her embroidery and greeted him with a smile. David was in her world now, and glad of it.

"May I sit down?" he said.

"Please do."

He took a seat and noticed Almira had a wicker sewing basket beside her on the daybed. From it, she took skeins of brightly colored silk floss and arranged them on the cushion.

Almira asked, "Doctor, have you seen Wigwam?"

"Wigwam?"

"My cat. He is a big striped fellow with white paws."

"No," said David, "but if I do, I will let you know."

"Thank you, doctor," she said. "I cannot imagine where he has gone off to."

She removed two strips of canvas from the basket, each a couple of inches wide and about a yard long.

"What do you have there?" he asked.

"A set of braces I'm embroidering for a friend. Would you like to see them?"

Almira stood and held up one of the strips against her plaid dress. Her pride was obvious. A colorful line of flowers had been embroidered up the middle. On one end was a worked buttonhole and the initials D.D. in cross-stitch, and at the other end the date,

1841.

"They're beautiful," David said, admiring the craftmanship. "He must be a very good friend."

"He was a very good friend indeed."

"Would you tell me about him?" David asked.

"His name was Daniel. He was recently a hired man here."

A tenderly worked personal gift for what sounded like an itinerant farm laborer. Odd. His eyes followed her. She set the braces down on the daybed. Then, in utter silence, walked to one of the windows where, standing at the panes, Almira looked out in the direction of the carriage house.

"Danny knew everything about horses," she said. "Everything you can imagine. He taught me to ride sidesaddle. And on pretty days like this, Mother would allow me to go riding with him. Father didn't like that. After Mother was gone, Danny and I could only go riding when Father was away and his new wife was distracted."

She touched her fingertips to the glass through which she looked, then turned from the window and faced David.

"Danny was to take me to a picnic party at the tradesmen's lodge in Willsborough Falls. He said there would be music and we might dance together." She wrapped her arms around her torso and twirled on the balls of her feet. "It would have been so gay."

The sight of her, happy and joyous, with skirts and petticoats awhirl, made David laugh aloud. This didn't seem anything like the sad young lady he'd first met.

"It sounds wonderful," he said.

Almira stopped still and dropped her arms. "It would have been, yes, but that wicked chamber-maid informed on us. Father was furious. He forbade me to speak to Daniel and dismissed him that very day."

"You must have been upset. Was your friendship with Daniel interrupted?"

"Yes," she said, walking to the fireplace and placing her hands upon the mantel. "Father sent me away to the academy that we might be kept apart. I still cannot forgive him."

David was about to follow up with another question, when he noticed she had no reflection in the mantel mirror, an unnerving reminder that this was a conversation with a spirit—not a flesh and blood human being. Before he recovered his train of thought, she spoke again.

"It's un-Christian to be unwilling to forgive, I know that," she said. "But something prevents me from doing so."

Almira pushed away from the mantel and turned his way. "Do you believe that God forgives all sin?" she asked.

The psychotherapeutic reflex he'd been trained in dictated he answer a question with another question. "You feel in need of forgiveness?"

"No, not in need of forgiveness, only unworthy."

Unworthy of forgiveness. David reflected on the notion. The thought left him feeling boxed in. He was unprepared for a conversation about the doctrines of Christianity, although it was obvious this question weighed on her. Feeling out of his depth, he returned to what was safe—relational psychology, a language he spoke fluently—and inquired further. "Why did your father object so strongly?"

She took her seat again on the divan and explained. "Danny had no means, you see, and he was a Roman Catholic. Father wouldn't have it. He said terrible things. He called him an Irish papist and a dirty stable boy."

David smiled at the irony, reminded of his own Jewish background.

She glowered at him. "You think this amusing, doctor?"

"No, no. I'm sorry. I didn't mean it that way. It's terrible when people in love are kept apart."

Almira's face turned from an angry scowl to sad relief. She cast her gaze downward, absently picking at the divan cushion. "Yes, it is a terrible thing. He will always be my true love."

They remained quiet for a few minutes. The conversation seemed stalled when David had an idea. He wanted to test her ability to track time.

"Would you like me to visit again?"

"Yes, very soon," replied Almira. Her mood seemed lightened.

He suggested Thursday. "That's in two days."

"Two days," repeated Almira, biting her lip. "Let's see. I think that I can receive you then...truly, the days do seem a blur."

David brewed a pot of coffee while he considered what was taking place. He had thought he was through with psychotherapy for good, but if he went on with these conversations, he'd clearly be slipping back into it, even if in a highly unorthodox way. But how could it be otherwise? Almira was the perfect intersection of his education and his natural interests embodied in one compelling, not to mention unusually attractive, young woman.

At the bookcase he retrieved his copy of the *Diagnostic and Statistical Manual of Mental Disorders, Second Edition.* He held it and looked at the cover. Using the manual was tantamount to taking Almira as a patient. Sure, she was a ghost, but she was by her own admission a troubled ghost. As ridiculous as that sounded, she deserved to be treated to the best of his ability. If she's a patient, these sessions had to be handled professionally.

Finally, David grabbed a legal pad and a pen. He sat down at the kitchen table, where he scrawled clinical notes—A. H., across the top in block letters. He regarded his handwriting, exhaled and got up.

"This is stupid." He got a bowl, dumped in some corn flakes, poured milk over them, and sat back down. Shoveling the cereal into his mouth, David continued to stare at the notepad until he finished. Then he wrote—

Background: A.H. is a Caucasian female of about 20 years old. She appears disoriented in time, though not place. Complains of disturbed mood. Openly seeking help for her dystonia but does not comprehend the therapeutic nature of conversations.

Picking up the DSM, he hesitated. David hadn't opened it since he'd cleaned out his office over a year ago. Doing so now didn't feel good. Cheryl Jankowsky's suicide, exhausting interviews with those detectives, Dr. Koenigsberg telling him he'd probably never become licensed. The memory of it was always a slam in the gut. His sinking guilt and shame screamed failure.

"Shit," he muttered to himself.

Forcing those thoughts to the back of his mind, David returned his attention to the DSM. There were over 180 distinct and separate disorders listed. That's a lot of ways to be miserable. A Sears catalog's worth. The way the diagnostic tool tried to superimpose a logical system over all this unhappiness was comforting.

Considering Almira was some kind of spirit entity, disorders caused by what was described as, "impairment of brain tissue function," could safely be ruled out. This left the psychogenic reactions, including Mood, Anxiety, Phobic, and Obsessive-Compulsive types, Schizophrenia, or one of the Personality Disorders. He wrote, "AH appears—always after dark. Very confused over passage of time. Seems unaware of time of day or day of week."

He reviewed their recent conversations. In the ordinary, psychotherapeutic world, some of her behaviors would have been aggravating. Her irregular schedule of visitation was one of them, to say the least, aside from the midnight hour of the sessions. *Alright*, he thought, *nobody said psychotherapy with ghosts would be easy.*

Yet he more than looked forward to his next chance to speak with his new patient—he felt compelled to do so. The idea that one could converse with a person from another time and reality was well worth the inconvenience of midnight sessions. That she experienced a form of depressive neurosis—insomuch as enduring spirits could suffer from dystonic psychological states like any ordinary person—made talking with her that much more irresistible.

David had also noticed idiosyncrasies in Almira's behavior. Most obvious was the way she avoided looking directly at him. Unless focused on her reading or embroidery, her eyes seemed always to be in motion, moving about the room, lighting on some object which existed in her time, then fluttering off to another.

Once, he'd seen her walk to the mantel and look at the volume of *The Young Lady's Friend* he'd placed there as bait. She'd made as to pick it up, only to stop.

There were other things too. For instance, she never asked where he came from or what he was doing in the house, and she never asked if David had seen any of the people who must have populated her life. Neither did she ask about any of those who populated his.

And then there were the repeated, odd inquiries after her lost cat. David speculated the cat was a transference object representing some deeper loss—a loss which was likely much more disturbing.

The aggregate presentation was of someone oddly disoriented. Whatever it was, there was certainly a quality in her which reminded him of patients he'd had with dissociative disorders.

In addition, the question of how aware she was of the external, present world consumed David. Whenever he was in the Quiet Room, she acknowledged his presence, but what, if anything, could she see from the windows—his truck parked in the yard, for example. Another point he wasn't sure of—did she move throughout the house? It didn't seem so. He'd never seen her materialize anywhere else, though there were odd moments when she felt near.

In order to assess her psychological state, he'd first have to measure her awareness. Did Miss Hamilton comprehend that she was a spirit—removed from the physical world she had once existed in? If not, then how did she reconcile their communication? Whether a symptom of some psychological reaction or an independent, comorbid condition in itself, wasn't her ghostly state part of her problem?

David refocused his attention. As it was, he simply didn't have sufficient information to hazard a meaningful diagnosis. Finally he wrote, "Situational Mood-Reaction, tentative, with dissociative elements," closed the manual and returned it to the bookshelf. The clinical notes David tucked into an old copy of Playboy, where Angela was unlikely to discover them.

Early in December, David Weis intended to shed light on a persistent question. How aware was Almira of material reality?

"Miss Hamilton," he said. "Tonight, I can see you perfectly well."

"Of course, you can," she answered. "We are together in my sitting room."

"T11hen you see me clearly too?"

"Of course. Yes."

"What do I look like?"

"You look like, well, ordinary, I suppose." Her vague answer had an avoidant quality to it.

David made a notation on his legal pad. "So, can you describe, for example, my clothing?"

"Goodness, doctor, these are peculiar questions. Is this a new parlor game?"

"No, it's not a parlor game, but it's important for me to ask you these things if I am going to treat you."

Almira's silence he took as assent to follow his direction. He wanted to test her awareness of modern objects around the house.

"Let's continue. Miss Hamilton, I imagine you walk around in this building."

"No, not anymore."

"You don't?" David didn't expect that answer. "Why not? Isn't this your home?"

"It is, but the other rooms have become uninviting. Only this room is as it should be."

"Uninviting? Can you describe what you mean by that?"

Almira took a deep breath, let it out, and said, "There is confusion and noises I don't understand. I don't like them. There are strangers too. A woman. She commands much of your attention when she is here."

That's Angela, David thought. *Incredible.*

From her fidgeting and restless eyes, David could tell these questions made Almira uncomfortable, but it was therapeutically important to go on. Besides, David had heard some strange things during therapy sessions over the years, but never a haunting described from the ghost's perspective.

"She's unhappy," said Almira.

He found the remark astonishing in its indictment, but David didn't want to mix his Angela life with his Almira life—not yet. Just the thought made him up-tight. "Let's talk about something else. Do you see anything on the mantel?"

"Candlesticks," she said, "and my book."

So, he thought, *she can see objects from her own time.*

He took a pack of cigarettes from his shirt pocket and placed it on the floor between them. David pointed toward it. "Do you see what I just put down there?"

"Only the bare floor, doctor," she said.

"Nothing else? Are you sure?"

"No, no," she said, irritated. "Nothing else. I've already told you that." Almira looked exhausted. She squeezed her eyes closed and rubbed her temples. "Forgive me, Doctor Weis. I do not mean to be cross with you, but I need to rest. I suddenly feel so very *de mauvaise humeur.*"

"Of course," David said, watching her close her eyes, fade, shimmer, and disappear.

Chapter 12

November, 1840

Except for her mother's funeral and burial, Almira stayed in her chambers for weeks. She took meals with her father when he was at home, but business had to be attended to, and more often he was away. When that was the case, Almira would ask Julia to bring meals to her sitting room where she picked at them apathetically.

French lessons with Mr. Descharmes were suspended for the present, as were her other sundry appointments. A few times ladies from church came to call, but as the Hamiltons were never active Presbyterians, the visits were interminable. Almira wanted Julia to tell them all she was indisposed, but this would have been unacceptable.

The last words with her mother repeated over and over in Almira's mind. If only she could correct her selfish act, to sit with mother and hold her hand until she drifted off to sleep. Only the most self-centered of girls would have done as she had. Only the most wicked of girls would have thrown the Bible against the wall and left it lying there.

A few times her father suggested she join him to visit Gloriana's grave in the grove by the lake, where she lay beside her children. Every time, Almira would feign fatigue or claim she felt a cold coming on. The fact was she couldn't bring herself to feel her mother's reproach. It would be more than Almira could bear.

Instead, she occupied her time in her sitting room, removing all colorful decorations from her clothing and replacing them with black trimming. The plaid ribbons, bows, and ostrich plume of her pearl-gray bonnet were replaced with black ribbon and a veil. Almira took apart her most threadbare dress. Using it for a pattern, she cut and sewed a new one in black bombazine, albeit with fashionable adjustments.

Preparing one's wardrobe for mourning was quite an undertaking, but Almira didn't mind. Sewing made her feel closer to her mother, as everything she knew about needlework had been learned at Gloriana's feet. Now, she would have to face the most challenging parts of a young lady's life alone.

The month of October flowed into November. As the nights grew long and the days leaden, Almira's need to be alone only intensified. Maybe she could sew her way through the grief.

One day, as they sat down for the noonday meal, Hamilton said, "My dear girl, Julia has prepared something special for you on this occasion."

Almira looked up. "Occasion?"

"Yes, your eighteenth birthday. Is today not the sixteenth of November?"

"In my sadness, I'd forgotten."

"I understand," Hamilton said. "We've been so distracted these last five weeks. Still, your mother would not have us let the day pass but we acknowledge your passage into womanhood."

Almira studied him, sitting among so many empty chairs. Much of his red hair was already gray, but he was, as always, groomed in an impeccable manner—freshly shaved, the hair at his temples combed forward in the style of a Roman senator. His dress was the same as it had been since her mother's death—a black cravat and vest, with the points of his white shirt collar jutting out from under his jaw, a black tailcoat with a black armband.

Hamilton played with his glass of Madeira, then swallowed it in one motion.

"You know," he said. "When I met your mother, she was such a lively girl. Her laughter would light up any room. She was ill for so long, I don't suppose you remember her that way, but I do."

Almira didn't know how to respond, or if she even should. Her father never spoke about his courtship of her mother or their life together before she was born. Maybe if she said nothing he would say more.

"Did you know," he said, his attention fixed on his empty glass, "that I proposed marriage to your mother four times?" Hamilton brought his eyes to meet Almira's. "Oh yes. The first, when she was fifteen. Her parents would not allow her to be promised at so young an age. Again, when she was sixteen. Again, her parents would not hear of it. When she was seventeen, I proposed a third time. That year, it was she who turned me away. When she was eighteen, I proposed once more, and she accepted. She knew by then that I would continue every year until she relented."

With the meal finished, Hamilton signaled for Julia to bring in the dessert, along with his daughter's gift. She came back with an apple pie and a package wrapped in brown paper.

Hamilton extended his hand. "This is from both of us, your mother and me. We planned this together while she still could."

From the weight and shape, Almira knew it was a book. She pulled the ribbon bow free, then unfolded the paper to reveal a volume bound in dark green with the title embossed on the spine in gold.

Almira opened the cover, releasing the scent of freshly printed paper. From the title page, she read, *The Young Lady's Friend*, by Mrs. John Farrar.

Hamilton refilled his glass and took another drink.

"The day before she left us, your mother inscribed this for you," he said. "She knew her time was near. The penmanship is uneven. She was too weak to write in her usual hand, but the words are all hers."

Almira turned the page and saw her mother's handwriting.

Beloved daughter,
Our Lord calls me back to his side where I shall soon be reunited with your sister and brothers. Though I must leave, let this book guide you in my absence. Allow the words to be my voice as you grow into womanhood.

Your loving Mother,
Gloriana van Elst Hamilton.

The sting of indictment hurt. Almira winced. It was clear beyond a doubt that on that last afternoon, when she'd been so impatient to go riding with Daniel, her mother had known she was close to death yet did not beseech her to stay. She clutched the book with unworthy hands and kissed its cover. Her father reached out and touched her arm, but Almira dared not look up.

"Forgive my weakness," he finally said and cleared his throat. "There is one other thing. Sandborne and Daniel have asked if you might meet them at the carriage house tomorrow after they've taken their noonday meal. I told them I had no objection."

The following day, after the hired men had eaten, Julia knocked on Almira's door.

"Excuse me, miss," she said. "Sandborne and Daniel request you come to them in the carriage house."

From the kitchen door, the weather looked heavy, threatening precipitation of some sort, so Almira put on her winter cloak and quilted bonnet. At the threshold, she dropped the veil to conceal her face before stepping outside. Cold rain fell as she came near the carriage house. Its wide doors opened to reveal Sandborne, Daniel and Ginger Snap.

"It's good to see you, miss," Sandborne said as she stepped inside. His voice was cautiously cheerful in respect of her mourning.

Almira lifted the veil of her bonnet and returned the greeting.

"Miss Mirie," Daniel said. "Me and Sandborne here have a gift for you. Come take a look."

Stepping closer she noticed Ginger Snap wore a new bridle and reins. The red leather was finely tooled and stitched, with brightly polished fittings of German silver, complimenting Ginger Snap's blonde mane and the rusty tone of her coat.

"Gentlemen, this is altogether the sweetest gift," she said, petting her pony. "It's so thoughtful of you."

"You're very welcome, miss," said Sandborne. "You and your father mean a lot to both of us, so it is our pleasure." Almira was moved by this humble and compassionate old man. Other than what he'd told her a few months before, she knew nothing about him—where he came from, who he was.

"Oh Sandborne, you've been so kind. If I were a little girl again, I should kiss you."

"You'll always be a little girl to me, Miss Mirie," he said, looking embarrassed by his words.

"Very well, then." She leaned in and gave him the tiniest peck on his stubbly cheek. His face turned crimson. "Mr. Sandborne, you're blushing."

The old man turned to Daniel. "Now, I am going to look for something upstairs. It will take me exactly one half-hour to find it. I want you to stay here with Miss Almira and be sure she comes to no harm. Am I clear?"

Daniel broke into a smile. "Bless you, Emmet."

"Sandborne," Almira said, "you are so sweet."

"Thank you, miss." Sandborne climbed the ladder to the hired men's quarters. The instant he was out of sight, Almira and Daniel threw themselves at each other.

"God I've missed you," they said in unison between kisses.

"Let's sit together." Daniel led her to a chair. Almira took a seat. He dragged a wooden crate close beside her, sat and took her hands in his.

"I've missed you so much," he said. "Are you alright? Your mother's passing must still be terrible. I too was fond of her."

Almira nodded, unable to stop her lips from turning into a frown.

"I've never told you this," said Daniel. "My own mother died of the consumption too. I knew when I first came here that your dear mum was afflicted and would pass, but I didn't want you to know."

Uncomfortable with the subject, Almira evaded it. "That was a beautiful gift from you and Sandborne."

"He's the one who put it all together," Daniel said. "I got the fittings. An old Dutchman in Moriah had a broken bridle, but the fittings were all intact and unusually nice. Sandborne went to the tannery in Port Kent for the leather. He cut and stitched everything. Come, I'll show you everything about it."

Almira held him in place. "No Danny. I've got to talk with you."

"What is it?"

Tears welled up. She had to compose herself before speaking. Finally, she began in a low voice. "Daniel, I have not told you this. No one knows this. But the day my mother died, I willfully left her alone."

He considered what she'd said. "Mirie, there wasn't anything you could have done."

"I might have. I don't know. She said there was something she wanted to tell me. She asked only that I sit with her for a moment and converse. I think she knew it would be our last time together. She begged me to stay, yet I turned my back on her, and now it's too late."

Almira broke into sobs. Her bonnet fell away, the impulse to bury her face in Daniel's shoulder impossible to resist.

"My poor girl." He rubbed her back. "There was no way you could have known. Your mother was sickly for a long, long time."

She looked up at him, her eyes red and watery, with tears streaking her face. "She might be alive yet today. And if not, then she wouldn't have died alone. That must be the cruelest thing, to die alone."

Daniel stroked her hair. "There now. Your mum didn't die alone. She knew you loved her so. She is in heaven with Jesus and the Virgin now."

"Daniel, there is more I have not told you. The night mother died, I hated God for taking her from me. I cursed Him and threw the Bible against the wall. I left it laying there with the pages open to the floor for days. When Julia tried to put it away, I forbade her to touch it. It was wrong, I know, but I exulted in my rage."

"You've since picked it up, haven't you?"

Almira nodded.

Daniel looked relieved. "Jesus forgives all things. You must believe that."

"I am beyond forgiveness."

"Never say that. He understands all things, and He understands you. Trust in Him, He is your rock, and through Him all is forgiven."

He placed his fingertips under Almira's chin and kissed her. He kissed away the salty tears running from her closed eyes. Ginger Snap snorted and stamped her hoof on the floor.

"See," he said. "She needs your attention as much as I do."

Daniel got up and held out his hand. As she rose to him, Almira was calmed by the belief she could safely put her life in his hands.

Together they approached Ginger Snap. Almira petted the white streak on her forehead and laid her cheek against it.

"How I've missed you," she whispered. The horse nickered. Almira sniffled, then spoke to her again. "Your new bridle is most becoming on you."

"I brought something you can give her to eat," said Daniel, handing Almira a small apple.

"There now, my girl. Do you like that?" She mothered the pony. "Is that a good apple?" Almira smiled, running her hands over the horse's mane and flank, happy to be reunited with Ginger Snap.

"She's become shaggy for wintertime."

"Would you like to brush her down?" Daniel asked. "I'll wager she would like that very much."

At Almira's nod, he handed her a curry comb. With it she brushed her horse's mane, her back and flanks

Chapter 13

December, 1970

A new kind of reality was coming to life in Willsboro. Being part of it was irresistible—engaging David intellectually, philosophically, sensually and, he had to admit, spiritually. These experiences, whether real or fantasy, seemed more important to him than much of his ordinary life. But compelling as everything was, the numbing cold made getting any work done on the building's interior nothing short of miserable. Yet he tried.

Even though David carried a kerosene space heater from room to room, his breath was a constant cloud before his face and his fingers numb whenever they weren't wrapped around a hot cup of coffee. It made the effort seemed misguided.

One night in mid-December, the temperature dropped to twelve below zero. Second thoughts came easily after two wasted days spent lying in a crawlspace, thawing and soldering burst pipes. That was it. As much as David hated the idea of retreating to Manhattan until spring, it made sense. He drained the plumbing, shut the house down, and limped back to his studio in the city.

He first visited his parents. It was an obligation, a chore. David's mother acted like a lot of women her age, preoccupied by anxious obsessions. His father's heart condition had grown worse. He talked incessantly about the rental property David managed for him.

"Someday soon that apartment building will be yours," he told David over and over. "It can save your life. It's income that will always be there."

"I know, Pop, I know," David repeated over and over.

A lot of unsolicited advice followed, mostly amounting to "Whatever you do, don't rent to blacks or Puerto Ricans."

Of course, they bombarded him with good news about his older brother's new house in Lindenhurst, his kid sister the teacher, and an array of successful cousins. The underlying message had something to do with his dubious decision to leave psychology and go into antiques full time.

More than usual, David's mother grated on his nerves. She'd look at him with one of those worried expressions. "So, when are we going to meet this girlfriend of yours?"

"She's another one of your *shiksa* nurses, isn't she," his old man said.

He'd had about all he could take of the bigoted comments. David made a show of slapping his forehead, conveniently remembering an appointment in Brooklyn.

Having made good his escape, David drove straight to his studio, locked himself inside and took the telephone receiver off the hook. Social withdrawal wasn't a particularly healthy coping mechanism, but it was his way until he could get used to the urban scene again.

Over the coming days an old familiar pattern reasserted itself. By day, he combed through the inventories of second-hand shops and the shelves of used bookstores or hit estate sales where he could sift through the bathtub ring of a stranger's life.

That was how he passed his time each day until Angela got off work. If she didn't have night classes, they went out. If she did, he'd wait for her in the library and they would get something to eat afterwards. Sometimes she returned with him to his apartment and spent the night.

Overall, he found this aimless life boring, and it left him irritable. He had far too much time to think about all the reasons he didn't like the city anymore. It was the city he found haunted, full of the ghosts of his failed career jumping at him from the shadows.

Compounding all this malaise was Christmas and Hanukah season. Not being Christian and only nominally Jewish, this time of year left David feeling like more of an outsider than usual, a cultural supernumerary.

On Christmas day he found himself alone in the studio. Angela had family obligations on Long Island. He could have—maybe should have—gone along. He was invited after all, but a holiday get together with his girlfriend's ginzo relatives wasn't appealing.

Listen to you. He rebuked himself. *You sound just like the old man.*

Alone, with no expectations of being with or hearing from Angela for several days, David felt restless and unsatisfied. He wasn't hungry but went to the refrigerator and stood at the open door. Leftover Chinese and part of a pizza stared back. Neither appealed.

He wandered to the stereo, knelt, and leafed through a stack of LPs on the lower shelf.

Maybe Bach's "Well Tempered Clavier" might soothe the mood. He placed the record on the turntable and let himself be enveloped by the music. The notes were perfect; delicate and precisely measured.

Doing these familiar habits initiated what, in psychology, was called a "behavioral repertoire." The next step required that he pour himself a glass of slivovitz over ice, settle in the chair at the window, and look out on the East River.

About to prop his feet on the sill, David noticed a joint Angela had left beside the ashtray. *Why not?* He thought. Nobody would call or drop in today. Quiet. No interruptions.

He struck a match, lit the joint, inhaled deeply, holding the smoke in for several seconds before letting it out. David waited for that familiar downshift of consciousness, the slowing of time, the accelerated onrush of one thought over another in parallel streams. He reflected on the situations of his life—the property in Willsboro, Carriage House Antiques, Angela's gentle but persistent pressure on him to make their relationship public, if not permanent and, of course, the supernatural conversations in the quiet room.

Time passed. How much time, David didn't know, only that he'd been listening to the snap and pop repeat at the end of the record for what seemed like ages. Getting up, he flipped the disc over and found his thoughts refocused to early 1969, February 3rd, a Monday almost two years ago...

Inside his office at Dr. Koenigsberg's psychotherapy practice, Maureen buzzed him.

"Dr. Weis," she said, "there are two men here to see you from the police department."

David got up from his desk to open his office door. A stocky guy of about forty-five walked in, flashing a badge. Another, younger man in a better suit, followed.

"Yes? Can I help you?"

"I'm Detective Sergeant DeCarlo, and this is Detective Boyle. We'd like to ask you some questions."

"Will this take long? I have a patient at four."

"Well," DeCarlo said, "this is police business. If they have to wait, then they have to wait."

"Of course, sure." David gave in, feeling intimidated. "Can I ask you what this is about?"

"Does the name Cheryl Jankowsky mean anything to you?" DeCarlo asked.

"Yes, she's a patient of mine."

"*Was* a patient," Boyle interjected. "She was found dead this morning."

The words felt like being slugged in the gut to David. "What happened?"

"We were hoping you could tell us," said DeCarlo.

"Was it a suicide?"

Boyle looked distracted, reading diplomas on the office wall with his hands thrust deep in his pockets. "C'mon, doc," he said without turning around. "You know we can't comment on that."

Stunned, David backed up to his chair and sat heavily.

"Doctor Weis," DeCarlo said, "Miss Jankowsky's apartment was full of letters addressed to you."

"What?" David's face snapped upward.

"Yeah." Boyle turned around for the first time. "All un-posted. She had them nicely arranged on the bed beside her body. We haven't read through them yet, but I think you understand the situation. Is there anything you want to tell us now? Something we ought to know about?"

"No, and I'm not sure I could anyway because of confidentiality."

"Listen buddy," DeCarlo said. "Don't screw around with me, just be honest. Were you involved with Cheryl Jankowsky?"

"No."

"Alright, but if we have to come back, I'm going to read you your rights."

"Look, I swear, she was a patient. A really troubled patient, but I never thought she'd do anything like this. And as for those letters, I don't know anything about them, except to say sometimes patients develop fantasies about their psychotherapists. I am aware she entertained some about me, but she was working through that."

"Well, she should have worked harder," DeCarlo said with a smug grin.

After they left, David took a Valium. If he'd ever had reason to take one before, the events of that afternoon more than fit the bill. He could sleepwalk his way through his last appointment of the day. Unfortunately, given the nature of the work, it was an easy thing for a therapist to do.

Now, high and staring out the window watching the growing shadows of a short winter day, David relived it all again. He had stayed at his office late into the night, ruminating on his now deceased patient. Cheryl Jankowsky, dead. A suicide.

Sure, she'd been histrionic, prone to manipulative and dramatic displays like all borderlines, but he hadn't thought her capable of this. And what about the letters? He'd been careful to keep everything professional and above board, but she could have written anything, even outrageous fantasies.

He recalled reviewed his clinical notes and been relieved there was nothing an ethics board could complain about, even if his therapeutic choices were debatable. Lapses of professional judgment can be foolish, but luckily, not necessarily criminal.

Stirred up by the pot, David's memories came back like unwanted guests crashing a party. He recalled meeting a psychiatric nurse for drinks after leaving the office. *What the hell was her name?* Later, at her apartment, things didn't go well. He was drunk and had trouble getting an erection. The rest of that week wasn't much better—a blur of booze, problematic sex and efforts to avoid Dr. Koenigsberg.

The cops had returned the following Thursday. They spoke with David in general terms about Cheryl and his work with her. David wasn't in trouble, but they suggested he stay in the city for a few more days in case there were any stray questions.

As the detectives left, DeCarlo leaned back into the office. "You know, I've read all of her letters. Man, this Jankowsky chick had some imagination, let me tell you. A genuine nympho. She was really crazy about you, doc. And you're a shrink, right? So maybe it would have worked out. Anyway, you don't know what you were missing."

David shook his mind back to the present, got up and returned Bach to the sleeve. He replaced him with Gottschalk. "Souvenir de Porto Rico"—the brooding, Latin piano piece was in harmony with his mood. He poured another drink and went back to his chair. The view from this window was exceptional. Straight ahead, in the narrow vertical space between two tall buildings, he could see the East River and part of the Brooklyn Bridge. Strings of graceful arcing lights shined in deepening twilight. His mind returned again to reverie.

A few days after he'd gotten the news about Cheryl's suicide, there'd been a meeting in Dr. Koenigsberg's office. Usually, he loved being there. Along with diplomas and awards, an array of black and white photographs covered the walls. Koenigsberg with Bruno Bettelheim. Koenigsberg with John Bowlby. Koenigsberg, one of a dozen young graduate students posing with Freud, November 1935. There was even one of Koenigsberg with General Eisenhower. David wondered why he'd never asked the great man about it.

"David, this is a serious and most unfortunate event," Koenigsberg said that day in his clipped German accent.

"I don't know what to say," David mumbled. Apologies seemed ridiculous but unavoidable.

The professor unbuttoned his sleeves, folded back the cuffs, revealing surprisingly hairy forearms and leaned forward, resting his elbows on his desk. He took off his glasses, rubbed a hand across his eyes, and said, "I'm sorry David. Your mistake is that you thought you were the only therapist who could help her. Of course, that was not the case. Your focus shifted from her response to treatment, to your fantasy as her unique, special therapist, which you were not. You became trapped by your own counter-transference, you see."

David remembered sitting, paralyzed with shame.

"This is, of course, not altogether unusual, no. Except, this time, the worst possible consequences have been realized and cannot be corrected." He held out an engraved cigarette case. David's hand had trembled as he took one, some imported Algerian brand.

They sat in the office, smoking. A clock ticked away the seconds. Koenigsberg shuffled the cigarette case around on his desk until he spoke. "I have to be honest with you, David. It will be difficult for the licensing board to look favorably on you, for several years anyway."

Koenigsberg let what he'd said hang in the air until the words and cigarette smoke combined into a miasma in David's consciousness.

"There is, here, I think, another factor," he said. "This has been a serious lapse of judgment—one that a more, shall we say, seasoned therapist would have been less likely to make. You may wish to reconsider whether you are well-adapted to clinical work, at least for the immediate future."

"You mean I should leave psychotherapy?"

"I mean you should take some time for yourself, David. Explore the world, inwardly as well as outwardly."

Hearing those words had felt like being brought before a verbal firing squad. His career as wunderkind psychologist died that day.

In spite of the slivovitz and marijuana, David's gut tightened as he re-lived those painful events. This was why he didn't like to smoke pot. His mind would often take him on long walks to places he didn't always want to visit.

Well, he thought. *Too late now.*

He recalled leaving Koenigsberg's office and dragging himself down to the sidewalk where he stood shivering and poised to hail a cab before another thought occurred to him. It would be better to walk, which he did. He walked for a long time. Block after aimless block, two, three, maybe four miles. Eventually he found himself at a bar in the Village, drinking and chain-smoking.

David didn't remember any more of what happened that night. His next recollection came the following morning. He woke up on Angela's sofa. At that point, they'd only known each other for a few weeks, a couple of casual dates. He hadn't yet been to her place on Staten Island, so when he opened his eyes, cotton-mouthed and bleary, David had no idea where he was until she knelt beside him. "Well, doctor, how do you feel?"

"Horrible."

"I'm not surprised."

"Is this your place? How did I get here?"

Angela laid a hand on his forearm. "Let's just say you called me from a bar last night. You were pretty drunk, so I went and got you. I would have taken you to your place, except you were completely shit-faced. I couldn't get you up the stairs, and I didn't want to leave you asleep on the landing."

"God." He groaned.

"I hope you don't mind, but I went into your wallet and paid for the cab back here."

A young woman walked into the room. She wore a short, terry cloth bathrobe and a towel wrapped around her head, turban style. She carried what looked like a space helmet under her arm.

"David, this is my roommate, Tina. She's a stewardess for TWA." Angela stood up. "Talk to her for a minute while I get us coffee."

Tina regarded him with suspicion. He tried to focus his eyes on her bright red toenails, then looked up with bloodshot eyes.

"So you're a stewardess?" David managed to say.

"And you're a psychotherapist," said Tina, sounding unimpressed. "Angela's told me about you."

A simple "Uh-huh," was all he could muster.

"Well, a hung-over psychotherapist on my couch. Far out." She walked off with her hair dryer.

Thinking back on it now, David still felt the sting of embarrassment, but the memory of what followed soften its worst edge. He remained on the sofa but had sat up. Angela appeared with two mugs of coffee. She sat beside him.

"Hey, David, you were pretty shook up last night. Is there something I can do?"

"Can you tell me what time it is?"

"Twenty after eleven."

David tilted his face to the ceiling and exhaled slowly. His breath was foul with the taste of cigarettes and alcohol. "Did I say anything I shouldn't have?"

"Nothing too bad, no," she said, taking a sip of coffee. "But why don't you tell me what happened?"

"What do you mean?"

"Come on," she'd said. "Something really rattled your cage yesterday."

The low hum of Tina's hair dryer came from an adjoining room. At the time, the sound had been soothing.

"Yeah, you're right, and it's pretty bad." David explained his emotionally unstable patient and her overdose of barbiturates. "I thought I could help her by denying the opportunity to romanticize our professional relationship. You know, forcing her to stick with the therapy."

David told her about how his deceased patient had become infatuated with him and his belief that he alone could talk her off the ledge of her desperate delusion. He told Angela about his conversation with Dr. Koenigsberg. How the learned man extinguished David's hopes of becoming licensed anytime in the foreseeable future, or ever for that matter. About Koenigsberg's observations around David's misguided countertransference, the comment about his maturity and suggestion that maybe psychology wasn't really for him.

"I'm sorry, David. And look, I know you're the shrink and all that, but she sounds like she was a pretty screwed up person to begin with."

"I guess graduating high school early didn't do me any good," he finally said.

That afternoon they had a long talk in which he told her everything about his life, his childhood, his teenage years and his recent past. Thinking back on it now with the perspective of time, he could see the classic psychotherapy of the conversation. Angela was good, a natural-born shrink. Whatever she lacked in formal training, she more than made up for with intuition.

By the end of the day, David had felt better. They went for a walk to get Chinese food. When the meal was done, he'd snapped his fortune cookie open and drew out the slip of paper.

It had read. "In case of fire: Be calm, pay bill, then leave."

Chapter 14

January, 1841

After the first of the year, the crushing atmosphere of mourning in the household lighten. Feeling simultaneously guilty and relieved, Almira asked the maid about it. Julia told her that Mr. Hamilton had instructed her to remove the black veils covering the mirrors and pictures on the walls. For him it was, of course, easier to be distracted by the affairs of business along the lake that required his attention. This included the supervision of a new schooner under construction at Willsborough Falls—the Gloriana.

Mrs. Hamilton's death had a greater, deeper impact on Almira. Lost, she went back to her needlework. The handling of needle and thread somehow blunted the pain. In her mind, Almira still heard her mother critique her progress. When Almira read from *The Young Lady's Friend* the words seemed to speak in her mother's voice.

Though French lessons resumed, and she began to practice piano once more, there was no joy in any of it. Almira often felt disoriented, and why not? Her guiding light had been doused in a driving rain of tears.

She missed her riding lessons with Daniel too, but from mid-January onward, there were brief periods when her father allowed Almira to groom Ginger Snap in Daniel's presence, provided the carriage house doors were left wide open. On those occasions, she would always ask Julia to prepare a bundle of treats for her pony—carrots, an apple, a lump of brown sugar. Petting the pony's nose and talking with Daniel as Ginger Snap ate from her hand was a delight, as were the kisses stolen when they were sure Julia couldn't see them.

In late March her father returned from one of a series of business trips he'd made to Plattsburgh over the previous three months. That evening, as Julia served the meal at a painfully empty dining table, Hamilton made small talk with his daughter. He asked after her French lessons and whether it might not be advantageous for her to be tutored in English composition.

"Would that include poetry?" she asked. "I should so much like to learn the art of verse."

Hamilton took a sip of wine. "I think so. Poetry is an important ornament for young ladies." He abruptly changed the subject. "Almira, there is something you need to know."

"Yes, Father?"

"I have remarried."

Almira blinked and felt dizzy.

"Yes. I know this seems sudden, but I assure you, it is not without deliberation."

"Father," she stammered. "Who? How could you?"

"She is the widow of a deceased business partner. Gerald Hackstaff of Plattsburgh. The name may be familiar to you."

"But Mother has been gone only since October, barely five months."

Hamilton corrected her. "A little more than six months, to be exact, and Loretta has been a widow well over a year. We didn't think it desirable to make more of it by announcements or a public ceremony, though we'll hold a reception here when I come back with her and the children next week."

"Children?"

"Yes. Loretta has a nine-month-old baby and a little boy, three-years-old, I think."

Feeling betrayed, Almira gasped. "My God, how could you?"

"Your mother and I had, for a long time, not enjoyed the full scope of marriage. I need not remind you of how ill she had been for years before her death."

As the implication of what he said became clear, Almira grew angry. She threw down her napkin. "I'm disgusted."

Their conversation was at a standstill, though Hamilton didn't seem surprised. Almira poked at her food for a few minutes and finally asked permission to be excused.

Over the following days hardly a word was spoken between Almira and her father. The tension felt unbearable, and only receded when he again left for Plattsburgh early one morning.

Like a powerful thirst, the need to confide recent events to Daniel came upon her. After all, she knew he was the one person who would understand.

Fortunately, that afternoon both Daniel and Sandborne took their mid-day meal in the kitchen. From upstairs, Almira could hear them and seized the opportunity.

Entering the kitchen, she saw Julia, Daniel, and Sandborne seated at the table.

"Good afternoon, miss," they all said. Julia picked up her bowl and busied herself with kitchen chores.

"Won't you take a seat with us, miss? Sandborne said. "Julia's prepared a right tasty stew."

"Thank you. That would be nice."

Julia brought a bowl and spoon, setting it in front of Almira without comment. The three continued eating until Julia began clearing the table.

"Thank you, Julia," said Almira. "It was wonderful."

Sandborne and Daniel agreed. Julia let it be known she had much work to do and stomped upstairs.

"There's more for me to do yet today." Sandborne pulled his smock over his head and put on his hat. "I'll leave you two to visit. Good afternoon, miss."

As soon as he closed the door behind him, Almira reached across the table to take Daniel's hand. He covered hers with his, enveloping it.

She whispered, "There's something I must tell you. My father has remarried."

"Lord, are you serious?"

"I am indeed. He returns from Plattsburgh in a few days with his new wife and her brood."

"I hardly know what to say," Daniel murmured.

"This is very upsetting for me. I won't accept her into this house."

Julia came tromping down the back staircase. Daniel and Almira pulled their hands apart before she entered the kitchen.

"Yes," Almira said, pretending to continue some earlier conversation. "I've read that as well."

Julia began wiping soot out of the glass chimneys of lamps she'd brought in with her. With no indication she would be leaving soon it was pointless for the two lovers to try to extend their visit any longer. Almira rose from the table. "If it stops raining, please do see to it that Ginger Snap is let out into the paddock."

"I will, miss, don't you worry."

Sandborne took the carriage to Willsborough Falls on Tuesday afternoon. He returned a few hours later with Mr. Hamilton, accompanied by his new wife and family, followed by a freight wagon. Almira watched from an upstairs window. Her father stepped down from the chaise. A little boy and a young girl jumped down beside him. They were joined by a woman in a dark dress, bonnet, and shawl. She handed a baby to the girl and took Hamilton's hand as she stepped onto the granite steppingstone.

Daniel, Sandborne, and the teamster unloaded the trunks and bureau, while the rest of the party walked up to the house.

Resigned that she must meet these interlopers, Almira checked herself in the mirror and made her way to the stairs. Even from the landing, she could hear her father introducing Julia to the new mistress of the house.

"And this, my dear, is my daughter Almira," Hamilton said as she descended the last few steps. "Almira, this is Loretta, your new stepmother."

Almira assessed her. Loretta was blonde, plump, an inch or two taller than her, and perhaps thirty-five-years-old. When she extended her hand, Almira noticed her nails were bitten to the quick.

"Welcome to our home." Almira offered a limp hand. "I presume this is your son?"

"Yes." Loretta pushed the boy forward. "Egbert, this is your new sister Almira. Do give her a kiss."

She bent forward and allowed the boy to approach her, receiving the toddler coldly. Then she eyed the girl standing off to one side, holding the infant. She was younger than Julia, wearing a cast-off, out of fashion dress. She supposed her to be Loretta's maidservant.

"This is Sally. She's here to help with the chores of the household."

The girl, perhaps thirteen, curtsied slightly.

"And this is Dorothea," Loretta said, gesturing to the baby. "She is but ten-months-old."

Hamilton offered an arm. "My dear, I'm sure you would like to refresh yourself. Let me take you to our rooms before I show you the rest of the house and property."

"You will excuse me," said Almira. "It was nice to make your acquaintance."

Back in her sitting room, Almira ruminated on every imperfection she could summon about her father's new wife. She was so irritated, neither reading, nor sewing, nor practicing piano could distract her from these thoughts. Late in the afternoon, she had reason to go downstairs and noticed preparations for the evening meal were being made early. "Why?" she asked Julia.

"The new mistress asked me to, miss."

"Oh, is that so?"

"Yes, miss. She says that taking meals at seven-thirty is too late for her little ones."

On returning to her rooms, Almira changed from her half-mourning mauve dress to one of full-mourning black. She considered wearing a veil to the table. While the dramatic effect appealed to her, she knew it would provoke her father's patience.

"This will be our first meal together as a new family," said Loretta as they took their seats. "I know little Egbert is as excited as I am. Aren't you, Egbert?"

Almira glared at them both from across the table, but when Hamilton expressed his hope that this would be the first of many happy meals, she brought her eyes down and said nothing.

Sally placed a mutton roast with applesauce on the table, along with a bowl of potatoes, and another of fiddle-head ferns. Hamilton carved the meat. While Julia served out portions, Loretta cut Egbert's mutton into tiny pieces.

"Claret, my dear?" Hamilton asked his new wife, once everyone was served.

"Oh yes, please, but do serve Almira first."

"I am temperate and do not imbibe," Almira said flatly. "But feel free to indulge your appetite for spirits."

Without acknowledging the biting remark, Loretta changed the subject. "My dear daughter, how have you passed the day?"

"I received French instruction from Mr. Descharmes this fore-noon and, as I think you must have noticed, attempted to practice piano afterwards."

"I did, and you play wonderfully."

"Thank you." Almira couldn't stop her tone from being curt. "I do think it important for a lady in society. Do you play?"

Before allowing Loretta the chance to respond, she turned to Hamilton and said sweetly, "Father, with the weather coming spring-like, I should like to resume my equestrian lessons. Poor Ginger Snap hasn't been ridden since mother's death."

"That will be fine," Hamilton said with an edge to his voice, "provided Daniel has all his work on the property attended to."

"Then you enjoy horseback riding, Almira?" Loretta asked.

"I do."

"My dear girl," Hamilton said. "Why don't you tell Egbert about your pony?"

With effort, Almira concealed her irritation, offering the facts concerning Ginger Snap without warmth or enthusiasm.

"We take a ride?" Egbert asked.

"No, I doubt that," said Almira. "Ginger Snap is not a horse for children. She is far too spirited."

Finished with her claret, Hamilton rose to refill Loretta's glass. "Well, perhaps Daniel would give him a ride around the paddock," he said. "Just as a lark."

"If you wish, Poppa."

Before he sat down, Hamilton spoke again. "My dear Loretta, might Egbert be excused? I think there is a matter of interest to the three of us which we ought to discuss."

Loretta turned to the new girl clearing the dishes. "Sally, would you please take Egbert to the kitchen for some pie?"

"Yes, ma'am." Egbert looked over his shoulder for encouragement.

"Go on," Loretta told him.

"Sally will give you something sweet for dessert."

Once they were alone, Hamilton spoke. "Almira, I will be clear. I expect you to afford your stepmother all the respect an honorable woman in her position deserves. We realize that our marriage may seem sudden, even a shock, but as I've told you, given our circumstances, a large, announced wedding would have been inappropriate, or at least in poor taste."

"Of course," Almira said, letting her absence of emotion speak for itself.

Loretta took a robust drink from her glass of claret. "May I say something?"

"Please do."

Loretta swallowed hard before speaking. "Almira, your father and I have known each other for a long time. My late husband Gerald and he had numerous business dealings over these last ten years. Your father has been a guest in what had been my home in Plattsburgh on many occasions, which is how I came to know and respect him."

She glanced at Hamilton and he nodded for her to continue.

"I regret that I never had the opportunity to meet your mother. She sounds like a wonderful woman and one whom I should also have loved for her goodness. When she passed away your father was distraught, but also a comfort to me in my grief for my late husband."

"Gerald Hackstaff was a good and honorable man," Hamilton interjected.

Loretta offered a slight smile at the acknowledgement. "I know you feel unhappy about the swiftness with which your father and I have married. There have been a few eyebrows raised, yes, but we saw little point in waiting to cement the bonds of friendship we enjoy."

"I congratulate you both," Almira said. "But perhaps you will extend your understanding if I feel my mother's memory seems easily replaced."

"No, not replaced," Hamilton corrected. "Your mother occupies a glorified status in heaven."

"Then I am mistaken and gladdened that you and Mrs. Hackstaff will have a long life to enjoy this bond of friendship you both speak of. Now, may I be excused?"

"Of course," Hamilton said. "On condition that you give thought to what we have said."

"Good evening." She couldn't bring herself to say what he wanted. She stood, pushed in her chair, and exited the dining room.

Lingering in the central hallway she heard her father say, "Give her time."

At week's end, a reception was held at the Hamilton residence. It was intended to introduce Loretta to her husband's social circle, but the affair wasn't well attended. Less than half the people invited came. Some obviously felt Hamilton's remarriage was in poor form, and those who did come were either there to stand in allegiance with an old friend, or driven by curiosity.

The latter were not disappointed by the spectacle. The newly widowed Hamilton stood with his widowed bride and her children, and all the while his sullen teenage daughter, dressed and veiled in black, sat off to one side.

When Loretta knocked over a glass of claret, spoiling Mrs. Hardy's dress, Almira made a show of directing Julia and Sally to "clean up the mess."

Later, after all the guests were gone, there came a knock at Almira's door.

"It is I, your step-momma," said the voice from the hallway. "May I come in?"

Almira rolled her eyes at the interruption and put down her book. "Yes, of course." Entering, Loretta placed the klismos chair a few feet from the daybed on which Almira and Wigwam reclined. Sitting sideways, she rested her elbow on the back and her chin in her hand as if waiting for her stepdaughter to say something. But Almira said nothing.

When it became apparent she would not break the silence, Loretta asked, "What is that you're reading?"

"It is titled *The Young Lady's Friend*. It was a gift from my mother."

"It's terrible to lose someone so dear to us, isn't it?" Loretta said.

"Yes, ma'am, it is."

"Please, Almira. I do wish you would address me as your new mama, that would please me so much."

"That was my mother's name."

90

"Very well." Loretta inhaled deeply. "Almira, I regard you as a mature young woman, and we aren't so far apart in age. Let's be on first names with each other, as friends are. What do you think?"

"If you prefer."

"That would be nice." Loretta twisted a strand of hair around a finger. "Almira, maybe I can explain something that will help you see that my intentions toward you and your father are sincere. I've been a widow with three children these last fourteen months."

"Three children?" Almira asked.

"Yes. My son Thomas died last November. Tommy was the apple of our eye. He was but six-years-old."

Almira saw Loretta's chin tremble.

"So, to continue, my late husband, Gerald left me with no means of supporting myself and our remaining children. Indeed, there was considerable debt I was not aware of. Since his death, I have been alone in their care."

Despite her mood, Almira felt a glimmer of compassion. She petted Wigwam, who had been sleeping beside her all this time. "Have you no family you could have called on?" she asked.

"No, my brothers and their wives have all gone to farms in Michigan. I know nothing of the farmer's life, and with my children I should only be an added burden on them."

"You seek refuge within my father's accomplishments."

"Yes," Loretta said, "but not only that. I do have a genuine admiration for him, and a friendship which has grown honestly. Your father and I both lost our beloved. We wish to be companions for each other in our later years. Is that such a crime? It is so very awful to be alone. There is, I think, nothing worse which we can be asked to endure."

"Maybe another glass of claret would soothe your loneliness," Almira said, dripping with sarcasticasm. "I believe there is still some in the house."

Loretta closed her eyes and placed one hand flat to her chest in a gesture of embarrassment and shame. "Dear child," she murmured. "Why are you so cruel?"

Almira petted Wigwam but didn't answer.

"Alright then," said Loretta, rising from her chair. "It is late, and there is much to do tomorrow. Good night, my dear."

After she'd gone, Almira gathered the cat on her lap and reflected on the visit. The way she'd gloated over Loretta's humiliation at the reception was shameful, and yes, it was cruel what she'd said to her tonight. But she could not help taking delight in cruelty. Why, she wondered?

Chapter 15

November, 1840

David felt like a caged tiger, pacing back and forth in his studio apartment. He'd read some great books. He combed estate sales and junk shops for sleepers and turned them over for quick profit.

He also spent a lot of time with Angela. Those dates frequently involved Chinese food and sex, but not always. Sometimes they would just read together. Best was the night she read Poe's poetry aloud. They talked about it late into the night. They'd had sex anyway, and it was above average.

But no matter how many antiques he handled, books he read, or intimate episodes he shared with his girlfriend, David's attention was often miles away at the house on the shore of Lake Champlain. It must have showed.

"You seem distracted," Angela said. "Is something bothering you?"

"No, of course not. I was just thinking."

"Okay. If you say so."

Early in the month, David could no longer deny it. "I'm going to take a quick run up to Willsborough, just to make sure everything is okay."

Angela couldn't spare the time. David didn't press it. His offer was half-hearted anyway, since the real motivation was to reconnect with Almira.

Back at Willsborough, it pleased David to see that Gary had been

111

plowing the drive all the while he was gone. After six weeks away, the accumulated banks of snow were impressive and much more than he anticipated. The place looked alright though; nothing amiss, no sign of break-ins or other mischief. He drove around to the back door and unloaded a bag of groceries, along with two five-gallon cans of kerosene.

David placed the groceries on the kitchen counter, then walked to the breaker box and snapped the master circuit back in place. The refrigerator hummed to life and the overhead light tinkled for a few seconds before staying on. The freezing house required that he leave his duffel coat on while he filled the kerosene heaters. Once he had them lit, he fired up the kitchen range.

Next, David walked from room to room, inspecting the spaces. All the windows were frosted over. Many of them had a quarter inch or more of ice coating the inside of the panes. A sleeping bag in one room showed signs of having been gnawed by mice. In another sat a half-finished mug of coffee, frozen solid.

Upstairs was much the same. Everything just as he'd left it in December. David checked each room, saving the Quiet Room for last. Scanning the interior, all looked to be in order—the klismos chair and cowhide trunk, the two candlesticks on the mantel and the mirror mounted on the wall above them. No, wait. Something was different— the trunk and chair had both been moved. Instead of being in the far corner where he'd placed it, the trunk sat against the westerly interior wall. The chair sat sideways beside the north facing window.

And there was something else, *The Young Lady's Friend*. He'd left it on the mantelpiece. It now lay on the chair as if someone had taken it there to read by the light of day.

Almira must have rearranged the room in his absence. With any luck, she would appear tonight or tomorrow. That would be about all the time he could stand in this icebox without hot running water.

Downstairs, he picked up the telephone and dialed his neighbor.

"Hey, hoss," said Gary cheerfully.

"Gary, I just wanted you to know I'm back at the house for a few days, so if you see lights, it's me."

"Sure, Dave. How long have you been gone?"

"Since before New Year's."

"Well that's weird, 'cause I thought I seen lights in your house a couple of times over the last few weeks. But everything's okay over there, right?"

"Everything's okay." After hanging up, he fixed a drink and spent the rest of the night sipping slivovitz and reviewing his clinical notes on Almira.

Without question, something was going on. Either he dealt with an actual spirit entity—a ghost—or he was hallucinating Almira and everything about her. Until he found real, incontrovertible proof that Almira had been a living person, he couldn't rule out either explanation. The chance that he might be hallucinating, psychotic, or was one of these multiple personalities he'd studied, remained unsettling.

Searching for an answer, David went into Almira's sitting room. He walked to the fireplace, lighted the candles on the mantel and leaned against it, looking around. Around the entire perimeter of the room ran a continuous stencil of Grecian urns and laurel swags. David's eyes rested on the empty chair. Placed as it was, it evoked the image of her seated there, watching and waiting for an eternity. For what? For whom?

The thought of Almira, so sweet and unsullied and yet suffering on and on was painful. Was it him she had been waiting on all along? He didn't know. But he might be the only person capable of saving her from this suspension between life and death.

He looked across the floor at her cowhide trunk. Could it provide an answer to these questions? Maybe if he examined each of the items again, but this time much more closely.

Kneeling on the floor, David raised the lid. Even in the dim candlelight, he could see the contents were all there, carefully folded and arranged—a perfect time capsule of someone's life, undisturbed for over a century.

He desired to unpack it, displaying the contents throughout the room as one would a museum exhibit. A memorial dedicated to Almira Hamilton, but something held him back. These weren't, strictly speaking, the personal effects of a deceased person anymore, even if she was just a hallucination. Almira was very much alive, in her own way, and now to him, personally. Handling her possessions seemed an uninvited intrusion, something dirty and voyeuristic. He closed the lid

95

and went to bed.

Three hours later David's eyes snapped open. A glance at his wristwatch showed twelve minutes after two in the morning. He pressed the damp hand towel he left on his bureau to his face, jolting him awake. No need for coffee. Trousers pulled on, he picked up his legal pad and pen on his way through the door and into the hall. To his excitement, lamplight glowed from under the door of Almira's sitting room.

David peeked inside, but to his disappointment, found her daybed unoccupied. "Miss Hamilton," he called, "are you here?"

"Doctor Weis, please do come in," she said in a clear voice from behind the open door.

He circled to see Almira settled on the floor. The skirt of her gray dress surrounded her, accented by an immaculate set of white collar and cuffs. She wore her usual coral necklace, and her deep brown hair was dressed in a simple bun. It gave off the scent of having just been combed with lavender oil. It left an immediate impression that she was altogether, astonishingly real. The trunk lay open, and she had already removed a few items.

"What are you doing?" asked David, his heart racing. Did she know he'd opened her trunk the night before? Would she be angry?

"I'm reviewing the things in my portmanteau."

"May I join you?"

"Oh, please do," Almira said cheerfully. "I have looked forward to a visit with you for some time."

David got down on one knee, his eyes immediately drawn to the dried and desiccated rose branch. Almira removed it and placed it to one side. To his amazement, the instant she touched the branch it looked freshly cut from the bush, with three pure white roses attached to the stem. Likewise, the trunk itself and each item within appeared bright and new.

Almira's attention remained fixed on the belongings inside. "I have so long wondered where my things could have gone. Now they are restored." Her eyes cut to him for a moment. "I think you had something to do with this, Doctor Weis. Is that so?"

"Well, maybe."

Almira's grateful smile made everything worth the effort.

"Actually, I found this trunk in the carriage house, and from the initials I knew it had to be yours."

"You were right, and how kind that was of you."

Almira took another item out. She spread her fingers across the black silk fabric and brightly colored flowers. "This apron is one of a matched pair embroidered by Mother and me under her tutelage, one for each of us."

"When was that?"

"In 1836, if I remember correctly. I was just a girl then, young and happy."

Almira took out a few books, smiling as she read the titles to herself. She reached for one that David remembered distinctly by the gold leaf flower and title embossed into the cover—the *Mossrose Album.*

"Is that an autograph book?" he asked.

"Yes, it's a memento of my tenure at the Albany Female Academy." She opened it and leafed through the alternately blue, pink, yellow, and green pages. Most of them were blank, but here and there ink inscriptions were delicately written. Almira pointed to one and chuckled to herself.

"What's so amusing?"

"This is a short account of a picnic excursion we made to Normanskill shortly after I arrived," she said. "There must have been fifty of us girls on that day, all from the First and Second Departments. We passed our time so delightfully, singing songs and frolicking on the riverbank. What a lovely time."

Almira's attention went back to the page. She read the balance of the note and laughed aloud. He'd never seen her do that. It was worth the trip north for that alone.

"Dr. Weis," she said, "you would have laughed to see those girls jumping from rock to rock out into the river, and their muddy feet and wet dresses when they came back to shore."

She turned a few more pages. Several of them had autographs written within the traced outlines of calling cards, positioned at odd angles or overlapping each other to give the illusion of depth. Some included a hometown or a short message.

"Eliza Whitney—she was a sweet girl," Almira remarked as her eyes scanned the pages. "And here is Susannah Platt from Plattsburgh.

Oh, Phebe Gardiner. Did you know she and her sister Mary are cousins to Miss Julia Gardiner, the celebrated Rose of Long Island?"

"No, I didn't," David said. "Were you very friendly with them?"

"Not with Mary, as she was already graduated, but Phebe was still at the academy and living at my boarding house. And here is Emily Wilcox. Miss Wilcox is from Orwell, Vermont and was fitting herself for a teacher. I shared a room with her. Did you know that her first name is really Thankful? Thankful Emily Wilcox. Can you imagine?"

David agreed that it was an unusual name.

"I should say it is," Almira exclaimed. "Terribly old-fashioned." She turned another page. "Now here is Pamelia Miles. She was from Michigan. I think she was consumptive."

Almira seemed fully immersed in her time—her strange amalgam of past and present all rolled up together.

"Would you tell me more about your life there?" David asked.

"My life there," she repeated. "At first I think I was a bit frightened. It was so new, and girls can be so competitive in their own way, you understand."

Almira returned the autograph book to her trunk and closed it. She stood up and strode across the room. As she approached the daybed it took on a completely solid appearance. Silently, she sat down. "Being with other girls of my own age was a tonic to me. We had shared interests, and I did not feel alone. If I had confided in them more, I might have felt more a part of their sisterhood. As it was, I felt loved by them, even if life there was not always easy."

David watched her closely. With Almira's chin propped in her hand she seemed absorbed in memories. "Most of the girls at the academy were from Albany, but I was a boarding scholar," she said, as if she'd been asked a question. "I stayed at Mrs. Bright's on Maiden Lane with seven or eight other girls."

"Do you remember any of them in particular, besides the ones you told me about?"

"There was one girl I haven't mentioned, my dearest friend Rebecca. She came all the way from Charleston, South Carolina. We became such close friends, like sisters. Would you believe she brought her house maid with her?"

This piqued David's interest. "Really? A black slave?"

"Yes, but she never used that term. She always called her a servant. Some of the other girls were scandalized."

"What happened?"

"Some not very nice remarks were made. Oh yes, how the fur did fly."

David's laughter caused Almira to smile. "Yes, Rebecca Carvalho. It is she above all the others whom I miss."

Eager to explore other subjects he posed one more question. "Did you find the classes to be very hard?"

"Some of them, yes. Algebra was quite incomprehensible for me— all the changing of the signs. But the natural sciences, those I liked very much. Once, in Biology, Professor Horsford exhibited a manikin, a little man made of papier-mâché so that it could be taken all apart."

"And did you have a favorite class of all?"

"*Oui. Mon préféré était la langue François.*" She beamed with pride.

"*Mademoiselle,*" David said, "*qui est en cour.*"

Almira threw her hands together in delight. "Doctor, I do so enjoy when you come to visit."

That was the last thing David could remember about their talk that night. He woke on the floor of Almira's drawing room, cold and stiff, curled up with his back against the wall. The breaking sun over the spine of the Vermont Mountains threw a beam of light against the interior. She still felt near, maybe still in the room. Trying to restore some circulation, David rubbed his arms and legs vigorously, then stood. "Goodbye Miss Hamilton. I'll be back soon, I promise."

Chapter 16

Summer, 1841

George Hamilton had come to the opinion that his daughter spent too much time with Daniel Dwyer—entirely too much time. True, he'd given Almira consent to be instructed in horsemanship by the lad, but these lessons had become frequent and lengthy. The situation presented a dilemma for him. He'd seen Almira suffer since Gloriana's death. Riding lessons were one of the few times he saw a smile return to her face. That sight brought Hamilton joy and left him reluctant to interrupt her short-lived pleasure.

As for Dwyer, Hamilton held a genuine fondness for the young man, and the emotion had only gained depth over the last three years.

Since bringing the boy home with him that day, he had never anticipated his daughter might develop affections beyond what propriety allowed. Hamilton wanted nothing but the best for Almira, and this didn't include her being an Irish laborer's wife, whatever the boy's character. Dwyer simply came from a class which Hamilton had struggled to break free and followed a religion he believed to be entirely incompatible with his family's future.

One evening as they shared glasses of port, he sought Loretta's council.

"Could you not simply dismiss him?" She offered. "Forbid her to have contact with him?"

"I could, yes," he said. "But Danny is a good fellow. He's no scallywag. To cut him loose in these times for no real cause isn't something I wish to do. Besides, it may all be innocent. Since Gloriana's death, Mirie takes pleasure in little else but riding."

Loretta suggested sending her off to a girl's school. "The Albany Female Academy is highly regarded. Did you know I was enrolled there during my own formative years?"

Hamilton frowned. "I wanted to keep the girl here to closely oversee her education." He sipped his port for a few minutes more, considering his wife's advice. "They will see she's instructed in all the important adornments?"

"Mercy yes," Loretta said. "Almira would be cultivated in every way and brought into contact with all the right circles, including suitable young men from good families she might never be introduced to here."

"You make a good point," he said, his hand rising to his chin.

Loretta held out her empty glass for her husband to refill. As Hamilton poured, she said, "You're going to Albany next month. Why not take the girl with you, have an audience with the principal and, if you find the school to your liking, have her begin there come September?"

Some weeks later a catalog arrived by mail. It described courses, tuition and boarding arrangements, but being still undecided, Hamilton set it aside.

All this changed when he returned home from a short business trip. According to Loretta, his daughter had twice ridden with Daniel during his absence, and both times they'd been gone for hours.

At the breakfast table the next morning, Hamilton announced, "Almira, I'm traveling to Albany on Monday. You will accompany me."

Almira looked stunned, but Hamilton had expected that.

"We will be gone for seven, perhaps eight days," he said. "I intend to discuss some business with representatives of Commodore Vanderbilt while we are there, but we'll also meet with the administrators of the Albany Female Academy to arrange for your further education."

"But surely you don't intend to send me away."

"Yes. We feel it would be a good opportunity for you."

"Did you know, my dear," Loretta said, "that I attended that institution?"

Almira's jaw tightened. "I did not."

"Oh yes. Of course, this is nearly fifteen years past. It's my understanding that since that time, a substantial and impressive new building has been erected."

"Almira," her father said, "this academy is well appointed. It calls for no small expense, but it will expose you to a social class not available to you here in Willsborough."

While packing her cowhide trunk, Almira brooded. This was all that intemperate Loretta's doing, she told herself over and over. Father had never before said anything about sending her off to school. The thought of being apart from Daniel for months at a time, unable to enjoy riding together, talking quietly, adoring and being adored by him, was unthinkable.

Yet, as much as it would hurt to be apart from Daniel, the prospect of living in Albany with other girls her age was exciting too. She'd never been to a city that large before. There would be finely dressed ladies and shops of all kinds, and trimmings for her wardrobe and bookstores where she could browse their selection of novels.

Late that afternoon, knowing Daniel was whitewashing the carriage house, she went to the adjacent paddock where Ginger Snap and the other horses were kept. She and Daniel could talk, keeping out of sight.

"I have bad news," she told him as he approached. "My father informed me this morning that he's sending me away."

"What do you mean?"

"There's an academy in Albany that my stepmother went to some years ago. She has convinced him to send me there, I'm certain of it."

"When?" Daniel asked. "How soon?"

"I think in September." Almira petted Ginger Snap's muzzle. "He's taking me with him to Albany on Monday to be enrolled. I'll be gone the whole week."

"Your father's trying to separate us?"

"No," she said. "He isn't aware of us."

Daniel rubbed his hands across his face. "I'm not so sure. Your father is a very smart man. Besides, people gossip. Julia and that new girl have their noses in everything."

"Don't be sad, Danny."

"No, I can see it already," he said, staring into the distance. "You'll meet someone there. Some fellow of means, with more—"

"Stop it," interrupted Almira. "Nothing of the sort is going to happen."

"You don't understand, Mirie, It's the way of the world. It's always been that way."

Shortly after dawn, Sandborne drove Hamilton and Almira to Willsborough Falls where they took passage on the steamer *Burlington* bound for Whitehall.

Aboard with their luggage, the vessel well under way, Hamilton brought his daughter to a bench amidships. He gave her a tutorial in steamboats, pointing to the various features on the superstructure as he did so.

The day promised to be very warm, but with the breeze refreshing, she left her parasol folded. Passengers approached them and Almira had to suffer numerous, tedious introductions. She'd been aware her father as a man of some success in the world of lake transport, but until now Almira hadn't realized how well known he was.

Hamilton became absorbed in conversations with his associates and Almira's mind wandered. She would soon be an academy girl. She and her beau could communicate by letter. There was something romantic about that. She would also be meeting other girls her age and maybe they could be friends. It wouldn't be forever—maybe a year—and when she returned to Willsborough, she would get so many letters.

The *Burlington* tied up at Whitehall. It was mid-afternoon by this time and would be an hour before the packet boat was ready to begin traveling through the canal to Albany. From the dock, Almira observed a long, narrow vessel, perhaps eighty feet in length—essentially a floating room fitted with a blunt bow at one end and a rudder at the other. The painted white vessel had the name *Empress* lettered across the stern in red and gold. Barefoot boys clambered all over it, carrying luggage aboard, tying some of it down to the roof of the cabin, and bringing other pieces inside.

"Father," Almira asked, "will we sleep on the boat tonight?"

"Yes," he said. "There are berths along the walls in bunk-bed style. It's all very ingenious."

With her father so experienced in canal travel, Almira felt more secure than she otherwise might have. When it became time to board, passengers lined up. Several gentlemen got on first. Hamilton and his daughter were next, followed by a young couple whom she watched with curiosity.

Once on the boat, the constricted dimensions surprised Almira. She guessed it was no more than ten feet across.

"Follow me miss," said a boy carrying her trunk and bandbox. A small doorway led to a long cabin. The carpet, cushions, and curtains surprised her. On either side sat a bank of wooden lockers, the tops of which served as benches. Above these were windows with slatted blinds, something she'd never seen before. All in all, the interior was brighter than expected.

Meanwhile, bare feet padded back and forth on the roof overhead along with heavy thuds. She assumed those were pieces of baggage. Above and from all sides, voices shouted questions and directions, while from below the gentle splash of water lapped the hull.

The floor—or deck, as Almira supposed it should properly be called—swayed slightly under her feet. After the stability of the steamboat she found the unsteadiness unexpected but caught herself on her father's arm.

"Don't worry, child," he said. "As soon as we start moving, the packet will be smooth as silk. The boy will take you ahead to the ladies' quarters. I'll get myself situated here in the dining cabin and meet you later when you're settled."

Almira followed the boy with her trunk toward the front of the boat. She was led through a very narrow corridor. One side sat a galley, and the other had been devoted to storage and, judging from the odor, a water closet.

The passageway opened into another cabin similarly appointed. A small table had been set up between the lockers. A vase sat at the center, holding a bouquet of daisies.

"This here's the ladies saloon," the boy said. "Pick any bed you want."

"Very well, I shall have this one." She pointed to the first bottom position on her right. "You may place my portmanteau here."

The boy stowed her trunk and bandbox within the locker. He lingered for an awkward moment before exiting with an expression of irritation.

A heavy-set woman seated closer to the bow said to her, "He wants you to tip him."

"Excuse me, who?"

"That boy, the hoagie. He wanted you to give him a shilling."

"I'm sorry. I didn't know."

"You're new to travel on the canal?"

"Yes, I am," admitted Almira.

"No matter." She continued the repetitious motion of darning socks. "I'm Mrs. Wynkoop, widow of the late Horace Wynkoop. Me and my children are bound for Schenectady. How about you?"

"Oh, I am Miss Hamilton. My father wishes us to visit the Albany school I will be attending."

"Isn't that nice," the widow said. Though cheerful she didn't seem especially cultured to Almira, yet her motherly expression set her at ease. Nodding to a runny-nosed child of perhaps two years at her elbow, Widow Wynkoop said, "This is little Barbara. There's a boy around here somewhere. That's my Frankie."

"I suppose we'll be shipmates tonight." Almira considered what it was going to be like sleeping with this woman and her brood.

"That's right," Mrs. Wynkoop continued. "All the way to Hudson's river, unless we're lucky enough to be carried off by pirates."

The cabin boy reentered with another trunk, followed by a younger woman—the one Almira had noticed as she boarded the ship. The woman directed him to place the luggage in an unoccupied corner and offered a half-penny coin. Glancing at Almira, the boy made an exaggerated display of gratitude and disappeared.

"Ladies, it is my pleasure to meet you both," the woman said confidently. Tall and thin, her jet-black hair made a striking contrast against her porcelain skin when she removed her bonnet. "I am Mrs. Ezra Rawson, but please feel free to call me Sarah."

Almira guessed she was twenty-one or twenty-two. What a relief to finally meet someone closer to her own age. "I'm Miss Almira Hamilton of Willsborough in Essex County," she said. "If you will, please call me Mirie."

The widow asked Sarah her destination.

"My husband and I are journeying to the falls of Niagara to honeymoon. We are but newly wed yesterday."

106

"How romantic," Almira said. "I've been told Niagara is one of the great wonders of the world."

Mrs. Rawson stated she would soon know for certain. As the three women arranged themselves, they talked freely with each other. Almira asked Sarah if her wedding was a large affair.

"Not especially, no," she answered, "but the gathering afterwards was. There was music and dancing and games past midnight."

"Games?" Almira had never heard of such a thing during weddings. "Please tell me of one."

"Well," Sarah considered, "are you familiar with Snapdragon?"

Almira had to confess ignorance, but Widow Wynkoop hooted. "I certainly am."

"It's very simple," the bride said. "Soak raisins in a bowl of brandy. Once they have grown plump a match is set to them. The object is to pluck raisins from the fire and eat them whilst they are still aflame."

Almira gasped. "But are you not burned? And do you not become intoxicated?"

"No," Sarah said. "You won't get burned as long as you're fast, and as for the intoxication, well...just make sure you eat enough of them."

It sounded like so much fun, yet playing Snapdragon sounded like it might offend Daniel's temperance oath.

Sarah placed a slender hand on hers. "You seem interested in weddings. Have you a special young man? Are you someone's intended?"

The question caught Almira off guard. In her heart she knew the answer and had hoped so many times for the chance to share her maidenly joy with another young woman, but doing so here and now on the canal boat would be taking an enormous risk. Almira blushed, her voice stumbling. "Yes, well...no, I mean, not...I cannot say."

"I'm sorry, Mirie," said Sarah. "I fear I've embarrassed you."

The ladies suddenly felt the boat lurch. Almira knelt on the wooden locker and thrust her head through the window. The packet was being pulled along the towpath by a team of mules.

An authoritative voice called from the stern, "Ladies and gentlemen. May I have your attention?"

Widow Wynkoop, busy wiping her little girl's nose, said, "You two go. I've heard all this before."

Taking Almira by the hand, Sarah led her through the passageway, past the galley and through the dining saloon, emerging on the aft deck. Most of the passengers had already gathered there. Almira stood by her father, while Sarah took a place beside her new husband.

"Everybody, ladies and gents," the man at the tiller said. "I am Captain Thorne, owner of the packet boat *Empress.*" A tall man, Thorne was well dressed in vest, cravat, linen duster, and a straw top hat. "This is an express packet through to Waterford. It takes a day and a night. We stop four times for fresh mules, and if you get off, I'm sorry, we can't wait for you when we're ready to leave."

Thorne let the information settle before he went on. "We have twenty locks to pass through. For your safety, there are a few rules you must observe. Keep your arms and legs inside the boat, especially when we are in one of the locks. Mothers, please mind your children and don't let them get underfoot. You may ride on the roof of the *Empress,* but when the bowman calls out, 'low bridge,' you must be careful of your heads and hats. And if any of my chairs are knocked into the drink through your negligence or horseplay, I'll expect payment."

A few of the other travelers voiced a halfhearted, "Here, here."

"Also, gentlemen," he admonished, raising one hand high, "remember at all times that we have ladies and children aboard. The *Empress* has a reputation as a polite boat. There's no gambling, and I'll brook no vulgar talk. We will feed you later. That's all. I hope you all have a nice journey, but if there's any trouble, come to me."

There wasn't any trouble. The mules went slowly—at very most—something akin to the pace of a man's brisk walk. Unlike the steamboats, which offered an entertaining combination of speed, noise, and constant mechanical activity, canal travel was uneventful. The men tried to occupy themselves by reading newspapers, playing checkers or debating politics, boredom made them restless. Almira found travel by packet boat most delightful. The smooth progress of the boat as it floated along allowed for the leisurely activities she was accustomed to, like reading and needlework, but with the added feature of a slowly evolving and often pastoral panorama. Perhaps most appealing of all, she could converse among the women without needing to shout over the sound of thrashing paddlewheels. But the real glory of the packet lay in the absence of the bone-jarring punishment that travel by stagecoach necessarily entailed.

Late in the day, as promised, a table running nearly the length of the men's saloon was set up with the wooden lockers serving as benches, arranged with a tablecloth, ceramic plates, and flatware cutlery. For the first time all the passengers, perhaps twenty of them, were gathered in one place. At one end sat Widow Wynkoop, her two children, Almira and George Hamilton, and the Rawsons. The rest of the table was devoted to the single male travelers—a collection of businessmen and more accomplished artisans. One among them was a Scotsman who was nearly impossible to understand.

Cold mutton and boiled potatoes were served. Being summer, it was necessary to keep the plates of food covered with a cloth, for the flies crawled over everything. A satisfying, if inelegant, meal, she could wash it down with tea and iced cider.

Seated opposite the newlywed Rawsons, the Hamiltons became acquainted. Ezra Rawson explained that he was the proprietor of a harness shop in Whitehall. This interested Hamilton a great deal, as did all matters of commerce.

"Have you considered business opportunities up the lake? I might be able to arrange conditions advantageous to both of us."

Hoping to fend off a conversation limited to men's business, Almira entered the dialogue. "Father, the Rawsons are going to the falls of Niagara to honeymoon. Isn't that wonderful?"

"Yes, we are," Sarah said. "I have been told by a recognized authority that it is one of the wonders of the world."

Afterwards, coffee and four blueberry pies said to have been made by Mrs. Captain Thorne were brought to the table.

One of the men remarked on the recent death of President Harrison and the National Day of Fast in his honor.

"I have a man working for me," Hamilton interjected, "who fought with General Harrison at Fallen Timbers."

"Is that Sandborne?" Almira asked. "I had no idea he was once a soldier."

"Indeed he was, my girl, and he has the scars to prove it."

When the meal finished, most of the passengers collected on the stern deck. A few sat with their feet dangling from the back end of the cabin's roof. Slow summer twilight was coming on. At her husband's urging, Sarah brought out a small guitar.

"What would you have me play?" she said, her fingers plucking across the strings.

"Turkey in the Straw." Ezra's request seemed a comical choice, but the Rawsons sang it as a talented duet. Obviously, they had performed this song together on other occasions. Sarah played a few more popular ballads with numerous verses. Most of those on the deck took part in the refrains. Almira noticed her father smiling at her when she broke into laughter at all the gleeful singing.

"Do you know Jessie, the Flower of Dunblane," the Scotsman asked Sara.

"I must confess, sir, I don't. But won't you grace us in any case, and I'll try to accompany you."

"Aye," he said. "I canna' help but sing it." To everyone's surprise, the sentimental Scotsman stood and intoned the song beautifully. His voice rang out across the waters:

> How lost were my days till I met wi' my Jessie.
> The sports o' the city seem'd foolish and vain.
> I ne'er saw a nymph I would ca' my dear lassie.
> Till charm'd wi' sweet Jessie, the flow'r o' Dunblane.

He sang all six verses, tears welling and streaming down his cheeks. An enchanted silence lingered on the *Empress* long after he finished and took his seat. Sarah patted the Scotsman's shoulder and Captain Thorne wiped his eyes.

Almira turned to Hamilton and squeezed his arm. "Papa, it is so beautiful and yet so sad. Why must it be so?

Chapter 17

April, 1971

Spring arrived and David returned, this time to stay—at least through to the following winter. Except for the kitchen, the office, and what was still a combination bedroom and living room, the house was in a chaos of remodeling, not to mention stubbornly cold, even in early spring. The outdoors was worse—with months of accumulated snow melting, he found it impossible to avoid the puddles of icy water. Walking anywhere became a miserable slog through mud. His neighbor Gary had warned him.

"Around here we have four seasons; summer, winter, more winter, and mud season."

A couple of weeks in, David promised Angela an overnight trip clubbing in Montreal in exchange for some help painting. Though home improvements were clearly not her thing, she agreed, but would come to regret the decision.

David had a single-minded focus on the building, painting, drywall, and spackling cracked plaster. He couldn't help it, he'd turned into something of a slavedriver, his mind always on Almira and the quiet room.

Angela couldn't mistake the indefinable sense that his mind was on something—no, *someone* else. Her sleep was restless with nightmares full of arguments between a man and a woman, angry shouts and crying. They were unsettling and stirred up unhappy memories about

Angela's own teenage years.

Once, after one of these nightmares, she awoke in the middle of the night, alone in their bed. The old house, now in the dark, spooked her even more. She called out to him. David finally tromped back into the room with a nonchalant explanation. He'd been "upstairs, checking on something."

No, it wasn't a great visit, and she never got her trip up to Montreal, but even she was too exhausted from remodeling to force the issue.

On her last night they got into an argument about the practicality of him making the lake house his primary residence. "I thought you were going to...I don't know, live up here one week a month or something. But now getting you to come to the city at all is always some big deal, and then you can't wait to leave."

It was a week before Almira reappeared. David noticed faint lamplight in her sitting room, but when he investigated, her transparent form was frustratingly unresponsive. He blamed Angela. Almira's distance had to have something to do with his girlfriend's disruptive presence and the tension between them during her visit.

Finally, late one beautiful spring night her lamps were bright and her form again solid.

"Good evening, doctor," Almira said, inviting him to come in and take a seat. "I'm glad to see you haven't forgotten an old friend."

David noticed how accustomed he'd become to her visitations. So unbelievable at first, they'd grown to be an ordinary, expected, and very desirable part of life in the house on the big, silent lake.

Tonight, her hair was elaborately dressed, with ringlets and the silver comb he'd seen in her trunk. "You look especially..."

"Fetching?" Almira suggested.

"Yes, that's the word, exactly. Fetching."

"Thank you, Dr. Weis." She offered a coy smile. "That is so very kind." Almira patted her hair, checking that every strand was in place. "What shall we talk about tonight?" she said as he settled himself on the klismos chair.

David had a plan. "Well, the last time we spoke you told me a little about your time at the Albany Girl's Seminary." He deliberately misstated the institution's name.

Almira corrected him. "I do believe you mean the Albany Female Academy."

"I'm sorry. Albany Female Academy." He took a sip of coffee from the mug at his feet before fishing for more information. "I've heard the school is located in very nice facilities."

"That is correct, it is. The building is a beautiful edifice on Pearl Street, in the Greek style, as you might expect for an institution of that sort. My stepmother was in another building when she attended, but that was years before me."

"What year did you begin there?"

"1841, in September."

According to her memorial, Almira died in December of that year. *She's rstyle, if you addan atribute [a dialogue tag] you don't need to use the italics)ecalling events from September,* he thought. *Does she exist perpetually in the last weeks of her life?*

As in their previous conversation, it wasn't clear to David if she understood these events as having taken place well over a century before, or as more or less current.

He tested her. "That was a long time ago."

Almira smiled, her eyes focused somewhere behind him.

David tried again, more directly. "How long ago was that, exactly?"

"Goodness, doctor," she said. "I'm not perfectly certain of that, but I should think...well...I'm not sure."

He made a notation about her confusion with elapsed time, along with a few other notes.

"You mentioned that you liked being with so many other young ladies your age."

"I did," she said, her tone full of enthusiasm. "This can be a lonely place, but never was I lonely there."

"So, what is this place like when I'm not here?"

Her face turned gloomy. "As much as I love this place, this has been a sad home of late."

"Why is that?"

"Mother is gone. Father is often cross, and I have little to say to his new wife."

"Don't you have any friends here?"

"No. The girls in this village are all dunderheads. They were unkind to me when I was a child. It is my belief they are jealous of Father's wealth, so I'm left here alone."

"Isn't there anyone you can talk to?" David asked.

"There is Sandborne. He is kind, but it would be unseemly for me to be familiar with him. Besides, he's an old man and there's little for us to talk about."

Almira looked down at her fingernails. "I do have two friends. Sarah Rawson, she lives in Whitehall. The other is my dear friend Rebecca from Charleston. She was an academy girl like me."

"Have you spoken with either of them recently?"

"No, it's strange. Though I write to both of them weekly, I've received no answer from either of them in such a long time. I worry that they are unwell."

The next day David called information for Albany and asked if there was a number for an Albany Female Academy. There wasn't, but there was an Albany Academy for Girls. He called immediately. The woman who answered the phone informed him that the school had no full-time archivist, but several volunteer alumnae dedicated to the preservation of the school's history. "One of them is here today. Would you like me to put you through to her?"

"Thank you. That would be great."

After a short time on hold, the receptionist's voice returned. "Doctor Weis? Mrs. Thelma Wade-Holding is on the line."

"Hello, doctor. How can I help you?"

David explained that he sought information about the Albany Female Academy in 1841. "Does your school have any connection to that institution?"

"Our name was changed in 1906, but, yes, we are one in the same. May I ask what your interest is in the school?"

"Genealogical research," he said. He told her that one of his ancestors was believed to have attended the academy. David didn't like fabricating an untruth, but he also knew a cold call from someone babbling about a ghost wasn't going to get him anywhere.

"That's a long way back," said Mrs. Holding. "But I'm very enamored of the school's early history, so requests like this intrigue me. You say her name was Almira Hamilton?"

"That's correct. Almira van Elst Hamilton. She was from Willsborough, New York."

"Excellent," she said. David could hear her jotting notes on paper. "I'll look into this and let you know what I find. If it isn't too much, I'll pop some photostats in the mail to you. Either way, you'll hear from me."

The following week, David drove to the upholsterer in Moriah. The rebuilt daybed exceeded his expectations.

"Where did you find this?" the old man who'd done the work asked. "I worked on one like this years ago, but nowadays I don't get to work on too many real antique pieces."

David helped the man load the daybed into his pick-up truck, hoping he wouldn't notice his lack of answer to the question. David thanked and paid him, grateful to have found an upholsterer he could trust for future restorations.

At home he had a difficult time unloading the daybed by himself, getting it in the house, and up the staircase. He might have called Gary for help, but he didn't want to make conversation with his neighbor just then. David's reasons for restoring the daybed and his impatience to place it in the quiet room were too personal for the questions Gary would likely pose.

By the time he placed the daybed exactly where he'd seen it when Almira made her first appearance, he'd worked up quite a lather. His first big sweat of the season. He thought this would make it easier for her to materialize. He theorized the fewer inanimate, supporting objects she had to manifest, the more energy she could devote to reanimating her living self.

Ten days later, a manila envelope appeared in the mailbox at the end of the driveway with the return address, Albany Academy for Girls, Academy Road, Albany. David's pulse quickened, anticipating that the independent corroboration of Almira's reality might be inside.

At the kitchen table he opened the packet. Inside, he found a letter from Mrs. Holding, explaining that she had reviewed the listings of graduates from 1839 to 1843.

"I did not find the name Almira Hamilton listed," she wrote. "However, I should mention that only graduates are given on these lists. Many girls attended for short periods and left or did not complete the course of studies. As such they are not listed here, though they may be listed elsewhere in our records. In case you have her confused with another relative or you have come across other names of girls she attended the academy with, I have enclosed this roster. Also included is a copy of our 1839 catalog, which I thought you might find of interest."

David got up from the table, clamped an opener onto a can of condensed soup, cranked the handle and dumped it into a saucepan. The letter was a bit of a letdown. Really, he'd hoped to find something concrete inside confirming Almira as an actual person. It sounded like what he had would be inconclusive.

Back at the table, David crumbled a handful of crackers into the bowl and started eating his lunch. He picked up the 1839 school catalog. The original looked to have been a booklet measuring perhaps six by nine inches, yellowed and somewhat the worse for wear being one-hundred and thirty years old. Notwithstanding his initial disappointment, the first thing he read was, "This Institution is situated in North Pearl Street, between Maiden Lane and Steuben Street."

It matched exactly what she'd told him. With interest growing steadily sharper, he noticed terminology Almira used when she described the school. Students routinely called Scholars and class grades described as Departments. The subjects for each were listed. He noticed algebra as she had mentioned, but also botany, chemistry, trigonometry, English composition, bookkeeping and philosophy, as well as Greek and Roman antiquities.

Impressive. Though the lower departments did devote two afternoons each week to "plain and ornamental needlework," this clearly wasn't an institution where sheltered and privileged girls were graduated as a mere formality. In fact, his impression was that the studies were rigorous and the bar of expectations high.

He started glancing through the list of graduates. The names Almira read to him from her autograph book were all there. The Gardiner sisters of Shelter Island—Mary class of '41 and Phebe class of '43. Pamelia Miles of Ann Arbor, Susannah Platt, both from the class of '42. Lastly, he saw Emily Wilcox, Orwell, Vermont, class of '40.

David felt thankful—as thankful as Emily's real name, to finally have corroboration that Almira once existed.

It wasn't irrefutable, but he was getting closer.

Chapter 18

June, 1841

Darkness comes on slowly in June. Several of the men took chairs to the roof to smoke cigars and sip whiskey, but the ladies all retired to their cabin. During their time on deck, the hoagies had let down their bunks. They found a roll of straw matting and a tiny square pillow. Almira couldn't imagine where all these things were hidden during the day.

"I wouldn't put my head on those pillows if I were you," widow Wynkoop warned.

A cursory glance revealed they were stained.

"Put your mattress and pillow inside one of your petticoats, unless you don't mind having cooties," the widow said. "You can wash it later."

She did as instructed, reaching up under her gathered skirt and letting down one of the several petticoats she wore.

On this summer night, even with all the windows open, the cabin became uncomfortably warm. Once everyone had arranged their berths and the Wynkoop children were put to bed, Sarah volunteered to fetch a few tumblers of iced cider. She was quickly up and through the curtain. Almira wished she'd thought to go along, but soon Sarah returned with three cold glasses already beaded with condensation.

"Ladies, try these," she said, passing a glass to each of them. "My Ezra made them special for us."

The widow took a sip and smiled, then took another, deeper drink. Before she tasted the cider, Almira smelled something unusual and looked at Sarah inquisitively.

"Are there spirits in this?"

"Only the slightest splash, my dear," Sarah said. "Remember, you must protect yourself from all the bad humors abroad in the night air."

Almira took a sip and coughed. "I don't think I can drink this. Besides, if my father learns of it, he'll be so angry—"

"Mirie," Sarah said, interrupting her. "You've heard of the ague, right? Well, you don't want that. If you haven't already noticed, your father is also busy fortifying his health, so don't worry about him."

Almira took another sip and held it in her mouth before swallowing. "It has, I think, nutmeg?"

"That's right, nutmeg, among other things."

Almira allowed the taste of the spiced cider to settle. "Sarah, you play the guitar so beautifully. Where did you learn to play?"

"From Ezra." Sarah laughed. "Now he's jealous. He says I play much better than he, which is true, but Ezra is the singer in the family."

"You and he are such a romantic couple."

"Thank you, my new, young friend. Now tell me, why are you and your father going to Albany?"

"He intends to enroll me at a girls' academy there." Almira's response was flat and without enthusiasm, which only raised Sarah's curiosity.

"Do you mean the Albany Female Academy?"

"I think so, yes," Almira said. "You know of it?"

"Sure, it's a well-known institution. But you don't seem overly excited. Don't you want to go?"

She shrugged. Almira wanted to confide in Sarah but was reluctant to share the least word about her and Daniel.

"Sarah," she asked, "we are friends, aren't we?"

"Of course."

"Well, there's something I've been wondering. Is it unusual to want two opposing things? I don't mean silly things like two different ribbons or novels, but big things—when we can't have both?"

Widow Wynkoop, who had fallen asleep, broke out with a tremendous grunt and snore. Sarah held her ears and whispered, "I hope she doesn't blow out the candle."

She reached across the cabin, took Wynkoop's tumbler, and divided its contents into their drinks. Almira thought that was hilarious, and her new friend, terribly fun.

By now, the night had grown quiet, and the men's conversations, though still audible, seemed strange, muffled, and distant. Sarah suggested that in preparation for their night's sleep, they remove their outer clothing.

After so much excitement, it was a welcome idea. Getting up, Almira felt dizzy and had to steady herself before starting to unhook her dress, but the task seemed impossible.

"Would you like some help?"

The offer of assistance was gladly accepted.

"Turn away," instructed Sarah.

She did so. Sarah pressed her hands against Almira's shoulders and ran her fingertips along the seams of her dress. "This is expertly sewn. I'm a milliner, and my sister is a well-respected dressmaker, so I know good needlework when I see it." She touched the black crepe armband on her sleeve. "You are in mourning for someone?"

"Yes," Almira said, "my mother. Early last October." Sarah didn't comment, so Almira continued. "Mother made this dress. It was one of the last before her death. I have altered the sleeves to be more a la mode."

Sarah stood, observing the slope of Almira's shoulders and the gentle curve of her neck. "For your complexion, this is a very nice color." She slowly unhooked the bodice.

From above, the bowman called out the warning of a low bridge approaching, and another male voice shouted, "Bend down. Van Buren men only!" An eruption of laughter broke from the roof above.

"It sounds like they are feeling their corn," said Sarah. "I hope my Ezra doesn't have a headache in the morning."

The bodice of her dress loosened as Sarah released the last hooks. Almira shrugged free of the sleeves and stepped out of her gingham.

"Now I can help you," Almira said, as Sarah turned away from her. She unhooked Sarah's bodice. She'd never touched another woman in this way before. When Sarah stepped out of her dress and laid it aside, Almira asked on impulse, "Would you like me to loosen your stays? Would that be too forward of me?"

"No, please." Sarah pulled a baleen busk from the front of her corset. "That would be nice."

As Almira eased the laces, Sarah finished her glass of spiced cider. "God, that feels better." She groaned, twisting her neck and shoulders. "It's been a long day."

She turned around and faced Almira. Placing her hands on Almira's shoulders, she guided her to face away. Sarah slid her long fingers between the laces of Almira's corset and pulled them apart, one by one.

"What is he like?" Almira asked.

"Who? My Ezra?"

"Yes. Tell me, please."

"He's like most men, I suppose, in most ways. He likes fast horses and cigars, and he likes to have a strong drink with his meal. Most of all, he works hard. Ezra has a kind heart and makes me laugh. I love him very much."

"I have someone I love very much too," Almira confessed. "But please don't repeat this to my father. I've not yet told him."

The men were mostly quiet now. "Give me your brush," Sarah said. "Sit here beside me, I'll brush your hair."

Almira felt safe, obedient, allowing Sarah to remove the pins and comb from her setting. Her deep brown hair fell from her head, falling in relaxed coils to her shoulders. Sarah began to brush it in regular even strokes.

"You have beautiful hair. Very dark and very thick."

Almira closed her eyes. The last time someone had helped her undress, touched her bare skin, or brushed her hair…it was her mother, and that seemed now to be a long time ago.

"Almira, do you enjoy writing letters?"

"I would," she said, "if only I had a correspondent."

"You do now. I will send you a letter from Niagara Falls, and you will tell me all about your academy school in Albany."

Almira looked up with a smile. "I should like that very much."

The young women exchanged places so that Sarah might now have her hair brushed as well. It was long, very straight and very black. Almira thought it like that of an Indian maiden.

When she finished, they agreed it was time to sleep. Almira lay down. Sarah blew out the candle and kissed her on the cheek.

"Goodnight, my dear."

But Almira could not sleep. Her head swam, if only from the unexpected kiss. She thought she must be intoxicated but couldn't say whether from drink or Sarah's attention. Besides, with the heavy curtains drawn across the passageway, it was terribly warm in the cabin. A mosquito whined in her ear, and after what felt like nearly an hour had passed, she whispered, "Sarah, are you still awake?"

"I am, yes."

"Tell me? What is it like, being married?"

"It's very nice," Sarah said, sleep overtaking her words.

Almira persisted. "No, I don't mean that. What I mean is, what is it like…being married…to a man?"

"Oh," she said. "I understand you now, my innocent sister. Being a man's wife can be a wonderful pleasure. Trust me."

Widow Wynkoop's voice startled Almira awake. "If you want anything to eat, dearie, you'd better get at it now."

She slipped into her dress. Her head hurt, her mouth was dry, and sharing the water closet with so many others was repulsive, but it couldn't be helped.

Back at her berth in the ladies' cabin, she took a handkerchief wetted with lavender water, wiped her face and neck and felt better.

Her toilet finished, Almira excused herself and made her way through the dining saloon. By now, the packet seemed familiar. Her father's voice greeted her as she stepped on to the sunlit deck. "Good morning, my dear girl. Did you sleep well?"

"I think so, even though it was very warm."

"Come, sit beside me. Did you know someone has saved a hard-boiled egg and the last piece of blueberry pie for you? They're here, hidden under my silk hat."

Almira thanked her father. She sat beside him and ate.

"Are you enjoying the canal trip?"

She nodded and flicked eggshells into the water. "It is sometimes a little primitive, but the singing last night was so much fun. I think it was like a party would be."

Hamilton chuckled and returned to the newspaper he'd been

reading.

Almira looked around for the Rawsons. They were seated together on the roof, hand in hand, watching the countryside glide past. She wanted to be with them—to be *like* them—but didn't dare intrude on their privacy, so she closed her eyes. Her mind wandered to what she would find at the academy. The girls there were likely to be from large cities like Albany and Troy, even New York and Philadelphia. Would they consider her a rustic without sophistication? Would they laugh and taunt her because of some transgression against fashion? Would she need to be guarded around them?

Searching for direction about how to conduct herself among other young women of her age, Almira went back into the cabin. Widow Wynkoop was thankfully napping. Almira pulled her bandbox from the locker beneath the berth as quietly as possible and found what she sought packed under her bonnet, *The Young Lady's Friend.*

Returning to the rear deck, she took a seat on a partly shaded bench. As was Almira's habit, she first turned to the inscription on the flyleaf: "In my absence let this book guide you." Studying her mother's handwriting was soothing but stimulated a sense of loneliness at the same time.

She leafed through her book and located the chapter dedicated to female companionship. Perusing pages, she found advice cautioning against hasty friendships...

The vivacity of youthful feelings is such that it often hurries girls into intimacies that soon after prove uncongenial and burdensome... nor should your confidence in their kind feelings ever lead you to make disclosures of your own affairs. They are not proper confidants for young ladies and should not be encouraged to talk to you of your beau and conquests, as it is a most unprofitable kind of intercourse for both you and them.

Almira considered the advice, and it disappointed her. Among the things she longed for most was the friendship of another girl her age. Someone who could appreciate the things that excited her interest, an ally when she felt peevish, company when alone and who could comprehend her desire for things she couldn't yet name. Someone like Sarah. Then Almira came across a most curious passage...

There is a custom among young ladies of holding each other's hands and fondling them before company, which is much better to be dispensed with. All kissing and caressing of your female friends should be kept for your hours of privacy and never be indulged in before gentlemen. There are some reasons for this that will readily suggest themselves, and others which can only be known to those well acquainted with the world, but which are conclusive against the practice.

What did it mean to be "well acquainted with the world?" She wondered. *Why is it so wrong of me to wish to be so?*

Chapter 19

Memorial Day Weekend, 1971

Angela had returned, and winter was finally over. Even if most nights still held a chill, the days were warm, with green shoots and sprouts emerging everywhere. Extensive, unanticipated hedges of lilac appeared all around the property, along with crocus and daffodils in unexpected places.

Carriage House Antiques was open. The augmented electric line wasn't installed yet. As Gary predicted, it continued to take more time and money than David anticipated. Still, there was a sign, of sorts, and the shop had a nice selection of furniture cleaned up and priced, along with dozens of smaller items.

He brought Angela's travel bag to the spot reserved for her. David kissed her. "It's really nice to have you back again."

She took a quick glance around. "You've been working hard, Doctor Weis. I can see you've made a lot of progress."

"Hey, thanks. The last time you were here, things were pretty rugged. I'm sorry about that."

"You should be. You worked me like a dog."

"I know. I'm sorry about that too. I'm going to try to make it up to you this time." He carried her suitcase to the bedroom. "Let's start with this oak dresser. It's for you," he said. "I won't put anything in it. And that Art Deco trunk over there is yours too, forever. It's cedar lined. I thought you'd like it."

Angela stepped up to the trunk and looked back at David. "Forever?

127

Baby, that's so sweet of you." She kneeled and opened the lid. A strong fragrance of cedar poured out. She ran her hands across the boards, then opened a small box attached to one side.

"Probably 1920s or 1930s, judging by the Art Deco styling," he said, the impulse to narrate the piece overwhelming. "It's what some people call a hope chest."

"Like for someone's trousseau?" she said, still inhaling the aroma of cedar. "I love it."

"As soon as you get your things put away, I want to show you something else."

Angela looked at him from over her shoulder. "I'll bet you do," she said playfully.

Later that afternoon, as they lay dozing amidst a catastrophe of blankets, pillows, and discarded clothing, Angela propped herself up on one elbow. "Wasn't there some other thing you wanted to show me?"

"Huh? Oh, yeah," David said, remembering. "Put on some shoes, it's upstairs."

Angela pulled on a pair of panties and David's white Oxford shirt, followed by her cork wedges.

"I like your outfit," said David, holding out his hand. He led her through the central hallway and up the stairs. "Remember that daybed you helped me pull out of the barn?"

"The one with the mice in it."

"Right. Well, I found this old guy in Moriah who does upholstery."

"I had a feeling this involved your special room."

"You know me too well," he said as he opened the door. "Take a look at this."

The daybed sat along one wall, its foot at the corner of the room and the single cushioned arm positioned near the east window. It had been reupholstered in sumptuous red velvet, with the wooden portions stripped and refinished.

"Get this," he told her. "This old man I went to, he actually had enough Spanish moss salvaged from junk furniture to stuff this with the right thing. Spanish moss is what they used on upholstered furniture back then. Isn't that too cool?"

Angela looked at him and shook her head. "You're a fanatic, you know that?" She meant it as a tease about his eccentricities, but David took it as a badge of honor to be so described.

"Go ahead. Sit on it. Try it out."

She did as instructed, testing different positions—sitting up, lying back, and a few other poses in between.

Leaning against the wall, David folded his arms across his chest. "You look pretty sexy doing that. I should go get my camera."

"You've got a dirty mind." Angela laughed. "But I like you. We're gonna have to try fooling around on this thing."

That weekend, a lot of the couple's time was spent sprucing up the property. Angela combed the yard with a bamboo rake. Feeling athletic with a machete in his hand, David concentrated on the overgrown areas. They must have filled a steel drum from the barn a half dozen times with dead leaves, fallen branches, and other trash to be burned. Flower beds started to emerge. They even uncovered a brick walkway from the front of the house to a large granite mounting-stone near the drive.

Around mid-day, Angela brought out a couple of salami sandwiches. She and David sat on the front steps. They ate lunch, flanked by large Doric columns.

"David," she said, "I've been thinking. This place has potential."

"Of course, it does."

"No, I don't mean as an antique shop necessarily. Check it out. This enormous old place? It could be made up like a camp for troubled kids. Have you ever thought of that?"

David didn't respond. Angela was a big picture girl, so hearing her come out with something like this didn't surprise him, but it didn't interest him either.

She went on, expanding her ideas. "Or even a retreat for people who need to get away from the rat-race for a while and maybe have some psychotherapy in the meantime. What do you think?"

"I think I'm done with psychotherapy, that's what I think," he said.

"Do you really think you can support yourself here off an antique shop?"

"Yes, if I can build up a good list of high-end dealers and collectors in the city, together with the income from the apartment building," he said. "As for establishing some sort of retreat, that would really take a lot of money—a whole lot more than I have now. Besides, I'd need to be licensed, or be in partnership with someone who is."

"Okay," she said, "so what's the problem?"

David could feel himself tensing up. "Look, Angie. I'm not cut out for psychology. In case you've forgotten, it didn't go well for me, and it went a lot worse for someone else."

"You're talking about your client, the—"

"The suicide."

"Look," she said. "You've got to stop guilt-tripping yourself about that. What's done is done."

David didn't say anything.

"So you're gonna give up."

"That's an ugly way of putting it, but yes."

The conversation went dead for several minutes. Angela took a drink from her bottle of Coke.

"It just seems like a lot of education and effort to throw it all away. I know you love antiques, but how many people really make a good living at it? You could support a family doing psychology with your degree. I'm not so sure you could, doing this."

"So that's what this is."

"Yeah," she confessed. "Sure, in part at least. Is that so bad?"

David threw up his hands. "Whoa, whoa, whoa. You're throwing a lot of stuff at me at once. Can we slow down a little?"

"Sure, maybe we can talk about this again later."

They returned to the much-needed yard work, but the conversation with Angela had thrown him off. David needed to clear his head, so he suggested they take a drive in the Karmann Ghia. An hour later they found themselves in the sleepy village of Essex on the shore of Lake Champlain.

"Hey," he said. "Let's take the ferry and check out Burlington."

The ferry wouldn't leave for another hour, so they killed time walking around the village. Essex looked frozen in time. Most of the village was composed of early nineteenth century stone buildings, built close on to narrow streets.

"God," Angela wondered out loud. "What the hell do people around here do for a living?"

"I think a lot of them work at the prison in Dannemora," David said. "Or the Air Force base in Plattsburgh. Some of them probably work in Burlington, across the lake. There's a pretty big university up there and a hospital, I know that."

130

The ferry ride was scenic. Seagulls soaring, and a rumbling diesel engine provided the background score. They stood at the bow. Angela tried to light a cigarette until she gave up and let the wind take her hair. She made a big show of breathing in. "This is really nice," she said.

It pleased David to see her enjoying herself so thoroughly. Maybe, he hoped, the beauty of the mountains and lake were growing on her, softening her self-admitted, superior attitude toward anything outside the five boroughs of New York City.

On the Vermont side, they parked. David pulled his road atlas from under the seat as Angela got out. "Can I get you a can of soda?"

"Sure."

David studied the map until she came back. The can was ice-cold. He pulled the tab off and pushed it through the slot, took a drink, then pointed to the atlas. "This is the route we'll take."

The route turned out to be a secondary road, one which rose and fell at intervals like swells of the ocean. "A roller-coaster," was Angela's comment.

Sometimes they could see the Adirondacks across Lake Champlain. The mountains in New York were taller than those in Vermont, with three and four progressively higher ranges visible, one behind the other and each more purple than the one before.

At Burlington, they ditched the car and walked around the downtown commercial district. Once they found a bar, they went in. They didn't have slivovitz—he didn't expect them to—so he ordered a whisky sour. Angela drank a screwdriver and smoked one of her long cigarettes. A lot of the downtown looked recently demolished. Whole blocks were missing. The bartender told them it was an urban renewal project. "It was a lot of broken-down old tenements," he said.

Angela got directions to the bathroom and left the table. Meanwhile David took the opportunity to finish his drink, replace it with another, and slam that down before she got back.

He considered the gouged-out heart of Burlington. No doubt there were run-down tenements, but it sounded to David like much of the original nineteenth century city was gone forever, along with its stories. He'd have loved to have had the chance to go through those buildings, rummage around their attics and cellars, read the graffiti written on the walls and scratched into the bricks, but it was too late.

American society obliterated its past without considering whether

131

the thing to be destroyed had value, if only by virtue of its age. This worship of the new and youthful; the whole culture was that way. And not just with buildings, but with people, customs, and beliefs too. The faith that there was always something good in the new, and that the new necessarily pulled us in the right direction, was shallow and simplistic.

"What's a good seafood place around here?" he asked the bartender.

He was given directions to a restaurant on the lakefront. Angela came back. David settled their bar tab and they went exploring for a bookstore. Finding new bookstores was a favorite pastime for them. Every one of them was unique and reflective of the town, with a Regional Interest section.

A paperback of *Toffler's Future Shock* stood out, neon lime green. He put it under her copy of *84 Charing Cross Road* and bought them both.

Half an hour later, they found themselves seated at a window with the perfect panorama—Burlington's lakefront close to the right, the mountains in New York rising out of the lake on the horizon to their left.

They talked about her classes at CCNY over chowder and crab cakes.

"Do you still intend to do your dissertation on Poe?"

"I think so, yes," she said. "He was a weirdo, and he had some pretty screwed up ideas about women, but he was a genius too."

David agreed, glad he didn't have to deal with academia anymore. He attempted to change the subject. "Angela, in Christianity, forgiveness is a big deal, isn't it?"

She paused on the piece of bread she was buttering for him. "Sure. It's kind of the central idea. God forgives your sins if you accept Him as your savior. Why do you ask?"

"I was just, well, I was reading this article in Newsweek about the riots in Northern Ireland, and the question came up."

"So..." Angela furrowed her brow, "...This is the kind of stuff you think about all day?"

It wasn't, of course, but he couldn't tell her the truth without divulging the visitations with Miss Hamilton. David wasn't ready for that.

Fortunately, Angela had more to say. "Tell me the truth. Are you seeing someone? Someone up here?"

"No, of course not." David hadn't expected this. "Why would you even ask me that?"

"A woman's intuition, I guess." She rolled her drink between her palms. "I'm probably just feeling insecure about us, that's all."

Their entrees arrived, redirecting the conversation. Over trout and lobster, they talked about his aging parents and taking over management of the apartment building. By the time the coffee came out, the conversation had turned to her kid brother. He had drawn a dangerously low number in the recent draft lottery.

"So, David," she said as the meal concluded. "You've pretty much made up your mind not to go back into psychology. Is that right?"

David looked out at the scars of demolition and construction across the Burlington cityscape. "I can't say never, no. Who knows what I'll feel like in ten years? I mean, I could always go back to it if I wanted."

"Maybe," she said, "but by then you'd be out of touch and out of practice. All the people who can help your career now will be dead or in nursing homes. In a career, ten years can make all the difference."

She had a point. "I know. I just need this time. You can understand that."

Angela reached for him across the table. "David, how do I fit into all this? I mean, if we were, say, just so we can talk about it, married and living at your place in Willsborough, what would I do? I don't think they need too many librarians or English professors on the Air Force base. And it's crazy to think I'm going to commute all the way here to work."

"Well…" David hedged, unsure of what to say. "Let's not jump to conclusions. You've still got two more years of grad school. Who knows what could change by then?"

His answer was a definite maybe. It helped defuse the tension of the conversation and served both of them well in the moment but was still evasive.

Their waitress brought the bill. David asked her if there was a ferry from Burlington to Plattsburgh.

She gave them directions to the ferry dock.

The ride across the widest part of the lake took much longer, more than an hour, but since they were now in Plattsburgh, Angela suggested they cruise by AAA Chinese to pick up something for the next day.

"Good idea," David said. "Egg rolls and Eggs Fu Yung for breakfast."

Angela placed the bag of Chinese food behind her seat. The night had turned damp and clammy, so David put up the top. It was much quieter now, and the aroma of Chinese take-out filled the car. Angela lit a cigarette. They could listen to the radio or talk had they wanted to, but their conversation petered out.

It was ordinary for David to be quiet, but not Angela. It was a sign she was brooding over something. Sure enough, as he turned into the driveway, she faced him. "What's this bullshit about Northern Ireland?"

David was caught off guard, despite his caution. "Huh? What are you talking about?"

"I'm talking about that stupid-ass question you asked me at dinner, the one about Christianity and forgiveness. You don't expect me to believe you're interested in that crap, do you?"

"Come on, Angie," David said as he turned off the engine. "We're tired. It's been a long day. Isn't it kind of late to get heavy?"

She got out and slammed the car door. "Don't put me off like that, Weis," she said harshly. "You want to know what I really think? I think you paid a lot of money for a dump in the middle of nowhere. I still don't see why you couldn't have bought a place out on Long Island. That would've been nice, but this place? Christ, there isn't even a decent pizzeria around here."

By the time they got to the back steps, Angela must have felt like she'd spoiled things. "I'm sorry," she said as they walked into the kitchen. "I shouldn't have jumped you like that."

"That's right, you shouldn't have," David said curtly, taking the offensive. "Look, if you're up-tight about something with me, that's one thing, but I don't appreciate being ambushed."

"I already said I was sorry."

David didn't care for her confrontational attitude, but neither was he ready to divulge his meetings with Almira. Fighting over why he'd asked that question at dinner would not make the secrets he kept any easier.

They faced each other for a minute. A serious argument could ignite between them if he didn't apply the brakes. "Let's just forget it. I understand how you feel."

"Do you?"

"I think so, yes."

His answer came off as patronizing. She challenged him. "All right, then tell me, how do I feel?"

David took a deep breath. "You're unhappy with my noncommittal attitude about our relationship. You feel frustrated and want me to get off the fence, make some public demonstration of love, like a dinner with your family—something. A real sign of commitment. Is that right?"

Angela nodded. "Yeah, that's pretty much it. So if you know all this, and you don't do these things, what am I wasting my time for?"

"You're not wasting your time, and I'm not putting you off. I just need to sort things out. Can you be patient?"

"I'm trying, but I can't wait forever for something that might never happen."

Except for the hum of the refrigerator, it was quiet.

"You know," Angela said, "sometimes, for such a smart guy, you're really stupid."

"Really?"

"Yeah, you're like a blind man." She pinched the bridge of her nose. "Look, David. Can't you see we're good for each other? You've kept me interested when other guys couldn't. And you have this love of old things which is kind of endearing. I like that. But there's more." Angela shifted on her feet and went on. "You know my moods. And I keep you from hiding at home. It's like I'm your lifeline to the rest of the world—you know what I'm talking about. But most of all, I keep you honest."

"What?"

"Yeah. You heard me. Sometimes you start spinning intellectual bullshit and I see right through it."

Her observation stung, so he let it go unchallenged. Angela had an insight which pushed him further toward internal understanding than he'd have willingly come to himself. *She's a natural psychotherapist.*

They stood in the kitchen for a long while, talking about their lives together and apart. David reached for her hand, but one finger was all she was willing to share. Still he held onto it. "Angela. I do love you. I know I don't say that often enough, but I want you to know it."

"It's true, David. You hardly ever say it. Why? What's wrong with you?"

"Nothing. It's not my thing."

She offered her entire hand. David took it and drew her close. "I've got to take care of some business at the apartment building. Don't take the bus home. I'll drive you back instead."

Angela kissed him and settled her head on his shoulder. "It feels rotten to argue," she said. "But I'm kind of glad we did."

Chapter 20

June, 1841

At Waterford, Almira and Sarah exchanged addresses and promises to correspond as the Hamiltons disembarked from the *Empress*. Two boys carried their baggage to a row of carriages. Hamilton tossed them a half-dime and instructed the driver, "We're going to Albany. Take us to the Albion at Broadway and Herkimer."

Traveling into the city, Almira observed an urban landscape for the first time. Row houses, first three, then four stories tall, presented themselves, singularly, then in clusters and finally in one continuous expanse. People of all sorts passed before her eyes—ladies in finery with their escorts and husbands, tradesmen, peddlers, a negro, and gangs of street urchins.

"We're here, sir, at the Albion," the driver announced.

The Hamiltons were shown to a suite of rooms. "Mirie," her father said once they were alone. "You may have any of your clothing laundered while we're here. And if you'd like your shoes polished and brushed, simply set them outside our door when you retire, alongside your laundry. The chambermaid will attend to it all."

Almira thought the whole situation luxuriant. "Papa," she said, "have I time to refresh myself before we dine?"

"Of course."

After a sponge bath and complete change of clothing, Almira emerged from her room feeling much refreshed. Her father had also put on a clean collar, shaved and buttoned on his finest embroidered waistcoat. The scent of mascar oil wafted from his red hair.

"Shall we dine?" He bent slightly at the waist and proffered his elbow, his expression full of pride at the sight of her.

Once seated, the Hamiltons were given the day's bill of fare. But Almira was preoccupied with the elegant surroundings and well-dressed society.

"Would the young lady like a glass of wine?" asked the waiter.

"No thank you. I don't indulge in spirits," answered Almira, discounting the previous night's spiced cider.

"Give her a glass of lemonade," Hamilton said. "I'll have a brandy. House will be fine."

With the waiter gone, he returned his attention to Almira. "I have no objection if you have something with your supper. You should try port, it's good for the constitution."

"Mother never drank," she said.

"As you remember her, no. But her health was much decayed in recent years. When she was young, we often enjoyed a glass or two together. In any case, people these days don't know how to drink."

That night was Almira's first meal in a restaurant. A new experience, but everything since leaving home had been novel. As she retired and lay in bed, she imagined telling Daniel about it all—the steamboat, the packet, the Rawsons and the singing Scotsman, the hotel, and even the plate of oysters she'd just shared with her father. But not the spiced cider. That would remain a secret between her and Sarah.

In the morning, Hamilton informed Almira there would be some time for shopping. They took a walk along Broadway. The amount of activity astonished her—carriages, people of all kinds, an omnibus too. Waiting at one corner for a gap in the traffic to cross, they noticed a sign on the opposite corner with several people gathered beneath it. The sign read, "Horsford & Cushman's Portrait Studio—Perfect likenesses by appointment or chance."

On crossing, the Hamiltons stopped among the gathered crowd inspecting a display mounted beside the doorway. The portraits of several people captivated Almira. Their faces were not an artist's interpretation, but rather the precise etchings of their images impressed onto silver plates. *These must be the daguerreotypes Daniel had been reading about.* And he'd been right. Though lacking color, they were not unlike mirrors in their faithful reflection of true life.

"Almira," her father said, "I want you to sit for your miniature while we are here."

"Will it hurt?"

"I should think not."

Overhearing them, another onlooker commented, "Me and my family sat for our miniatures last week, sir. I assure you, the process is altogether painless."

"Very well," Hamilton said. "You will sit for your portrait at once."

Almira folded her parasol and entered the building with her father. A sign directed them to the top floor. They climbed a steep, winding staircase. Another couple descended, forcing them to wait to one side.

"My wife and I have just sat for our wedding portrait," said the man as they joined the Hamiltons on the landing. "This is the happiest day of my life."

"Accept my congratulations, sir." Hamilton clapped the man on the back.

Though the bride chided him for embarrassing her, the happy husband continued, "But darling, it's true. Now I can remember you on this day forever, exactly as you are now."

At the fourth, uppermost floor, the Hamiltons entered a showroom where numerous examples of Daguerreian art were displayed. Despite the open windows it was very warm, and the establishment exuded an odd chemical odor. A young man wearing a white cotton tailcoat of window-pane check approached them.

"Good morning, sir," he said with a British accent. "I am Mr. Meade. May I help you?"

"Yes." Hamilton placed his hand on Almira's back. "I want my daughter to sit for her portrait."

"Excellent. Mr. Cushman is just finishing with another patron. If you like, he will be ready to create your daughter's miniature in a few minutes." Turning his attention to Almira, he added, "With such a beautiful subject, it must be a most beautiful portrait."

Hamilton ignored the fawning compliment. "Where is this Horsford?"

"Professor Horsford is an instructor at the Albany Female Academy," said Meade. "His duties there require his presence most days. Though he oversees the chemical aspects, it is Mr. Cushman who captures the artistic expression."

"Did you hear that, my dear girl," he said to Almira. "This fellow Horsford is a professor at the academy."

Visions of the scientist in Mary Shelly's novel, *Frankenstein, or The Modern Prometheus*, flashed through her mind.

Heedless of waiting for his daughter's response, Hamilton continued his discourse. "Very well. How long will this take?"

"Today we have a bright sun. The exposure will go quickly. I would estimate within an hour of the sitting you will have a finished daguerreotype."

Hamilton and Almira listened as the young man explained the selection of portrait sizes. Between glances in Almira's direction, he described the miniatures as sealed within cases of red Moroccan leather, appointed with brass latches and cushions of crimson silk.

"Prepare a plate for the girl," Hamilton instructed.

"Excellent, sir."

Almira walked to the window and looked out on the street below. Despite all the activity, her mind drifted to Sarah and Ezra Rawson. What were they doing now? Were they far away—Herkimer, Rochester? She had no real idea. Would she and Daniel ever see each other again?

And what was Daniel doing now? Grooming the horses? Whitewashing the carriage house? Maybe thinking of her too?

Hamilton browsed the images on the walls, fascinated by the invention which could seemingly capture a person's very essence in miniature. Eventually, his gaze lingered on a selection of postmortem portraits of the deceased in their caskets, on their deathbeds, or, in one case, a child cradled in a grieving mother's arms. How he wished he had such a token to remember Gloriana's face or to represent the emptiness they both felt when their youngest children were lost. Life was so fragile. It was so much the better to record his only surviving daughter's youthful vigor forever, while it was still possible.

"Young man," he said, gesturing for Meade's attention. "How are these portraits in death accomplished? Surely they're not done here."

"No, sir, they aren't," Meade said. "In those cases, Mr. Cushman brings his apparatus to the home. The lighting is not so good, but since the subjects are, well, quite stationary, we can allow the plate to be exposed for however long the situation requires."

Hamilton looked at his daughter. How he adored her. The knowledge that he would soon always be able to see Almira's face, wherever she was, or whatever the future held, was calming. Taking a seat beside her on the settee, he placed his hand upon hers. It was so pale and soft—birdlike in comparison to his, which was large and meaty. Though the last twenty years had not been physically demanding, his hands still bore all the callouses and scars of a youth filled with hard labor and exposure to the elements.

Meade emerged from a back room and approached the Hamiltons.

"Sir, Mr. Cushman is ready for your daughter's sitting. Please follow me."

He led the pair through a doorway, past a room that was certainly the source of the unusual smells, then up another, shorter stairway. It brought them out to a room on the roof of the building, mostly glass enclosed, with a skylight and windows on three sides and above. The height and strange surroundings amplified Almira's apprehension, leaving her feeling a little dizzy.

A pale man wearing a linen frock coat got up from his chair and stepped forward. In a fragile voice he introduced himself.

"I'm Thomas Cushman."

"George Hamilton of Essex County. This is my daughter, Almira."

"Miss Hamilton," he said, taking her offered hand.

He trembled, leaving her with the impression he was in poor health. Cushman led her to a chair placed before an unadorned backdrop. He asked her to sit down and rest her elbows on the arms. White panels were placed strategically at each side to reflect sunlight. Opposite, about ten feet away, was a wooden box appointed with brass fittings and a lens in front.

"Sir, is that box what they call the camera?" her Father asked.

"It is indeed," Cushman said. To Almira, he instructed, "Miss, young Sam here is going to hold a reflecting panel near you. Try not to be distracted by it."

A negro boy approached, carrying what she supposed was a sheet of cardboard painted with whitewash. Almira squinted. She raised a laced hand to shield her eyes from the glare. "Might I keep my bonnet on? The sunlight is so strong."

"I think that will be good," Cushman said. "Your bonnet will diffuse the rays of light, and it looks quite fetching on you. Now, you must hold yourself absolutely still for thirty seconds. During that time, keep your eyes fixed on this point here, just below the lens. Try not to breathe and don't blink. Relax and be at ease when I begin counting." The artist took up position beside his camera, holding a watch he'd pulled from his waistcoat. "Are you ready?"

Almira nodded, feeling like she stared into the muzzle of a firearm. Would there be a loud report, a startling flash? Too late, for by this time she was already afraid to interrupt with another question. Cushman removed the lens cap and began his measured counting.

"Five seconds…ten seconds…fifteen. You're doing very well, miss. Twenty seconds."

When he was done, Cushman covered the lens and slipped the watch back into his pocket. "All done. Now that didn't hurt at all, did it?"

The sign above the door read, "Mrs. R. Kendall—Fashionable Dresses to Order." Small bells announced their entry into the long, narrow shop. "Madam," Hamilton said to the proprietress, "I wish you to fit my daughter for a dress. Have her measured for something nice, but not too dear. Something sensible that would be proper at an academy. I have business I must attend to, and I'll return for her in three hours' time."

Alone with Mrs. Kendall in her dress shop, Almira took in the interior. It was intoxicating to see this collection of colors, textiles and icons of fashion, all in one place.

"Tell me," said Mrs. Kendall. "What is your desire?"

"As you may have heard my father say, I require something which will be proper and practical for daily wear in a classroom."

"You are attending the Female Academy?"

"Yes," Almira said, "I expect to, but not until this autumn."

"Very well. I've had many young ladies from that fine institution trade with me, so I'm quite familiar with their requirements." Leading her customer to a series of fashion plates pinned to one wall, Mrs. Kendall explained, "These are some of the latest fashionable dresses for girls of your age. Though they are inspired by the French mode, the exaggerations have been tamed for American sensibilities."

Almira scrutinized the pictures—demure ladies with tilted heads and long, insect-like arms. She noticed that darker, somber colors predominated and the style in sleeves was smooth—without gathering or plaiting of any kind.

"Here." The dressmaker pointed to one fashion plate. "This might be to your taste. It is smart and can be detailed as you please."

"I do like this style. If one were to make this up, what would the cloth be? Could it be made in a gay silk taffeta?"

Mrs. Kendall surveyed her stock of textiles. "It could be anything you like. It would make up nicely in taffeta, yes, but that might not be so practical for daily wear in a classroom." She unpinned the plate from the wall and brought Almira to a shelf across the shop. "These goods are a very fine wool—silk *cassinette*. It wears like iron, yet, as you can feel for yourself, it has a delicate hand. It's also very warm, which I do think would be to your advantage if what the girls tell me about the academy is true."

What else had they told her about life at the academy? Were the courses very hard? Were the girls nice, like Sarah, or were they jealous, petty, and backbiting? She must remember to ask before she left. As Almira considered all this, she ran her hands across the bolt of cloth. It was smooth like satin, gray with tiny green leaves woven throughout.

"I have two other bolts if you wish to see them, but this color compliments you very nicely."

"Have you a looking glass?" Almira asked.

Mrs. Kendall took the bolt from the shelf. She posed Almira before a long mirror, unwound a length of fabric and draped it around her young customer's shoulders. "See how it brings out your eyes?" she said. "And your coral necklace is perfect with this fabric."

Complimented on her wise decision and taste, Almira was shown to a room at the back of the shop and instructed to emerge wearing only her foundation garments. Measurements were taken by a crew of young girls in smocks and day-caps. Mrs. Kendall supervised it all with the confidence of a sergeant-major, jotting down measurements and notes with a pencil.

Finally, having dressed again, Almira was escorted back to the showroom. "When might the dress be ready?"

"We'll have it finished for you by the end of this week."

"Oh dear," sighed Almira, hand to chin. "I'm afraid I must return to Willsborough before then."

"Very well," the dressmaker said. "You say you and your father are staying at the Albion? I can have it sent there by tomorrow evening."

The bells of the shop door jingled. "Has my daughter been well taken care of?" Hamilton's voice was deep and protective.

"I think so, sir," the dressmaker said. "What does the lady think?"

"Father, Mrs. Kendall is sewing me a magnificent new frock. It is silk and wool and deliciously fashionable, but altogether sensible."

The next morning Almira woke early. As her father had predicted, she discovered her extra chemise and petticoats were laundered fresh and her patent leather pumps polished to a mirror finish.

She took extra care removing the curling papers from her hair, dressed it carefully and scented it with lavender. Her finest plaid silk dress, her coral necklace, lace pelisse and fingerless mitts made the ensemble complete. Still, Almira felt nervous. Pretty enough? Smart enough? She couldn't say.

It was a short ride from the Albion to the school on North Pearl Street. Though flanked by churches and other elegant buildings, it was obvious which structure housed the school. Its purpose as a temple of learning was amply displayed by the classical architecture. From the carriage, Almira scanned its facade. The building was impressive—and intimidating. Marble steps ascended to a portico upon which six large Ionic columns stood, perhaps forty feet tall. It was, in fact, reminiscent of her home in Willsborough, except that every feature was on a massive scale.

Almira and her father climbed down from the carriage. Hamilton paid the driver, instructing him to return in two hours.

Two girls of about her own age exited the building and descended the steps. They walked arm in arm, deep in conversation. Almira studied them surreptitiously. Upon reaching street level, they looked directly at her but said nothing.

Hamilton asked, "Ladies, can you direct us to the academy's offices?"

One of them pointed to the building. "You will find them inside, sir, on the second floor."

He thanked them. Almira curtsied in acknowledgement of their help. As they walked off, she noticed both girls looking back at her, over their shoulders. One whispered in the other's ear. Almira feared the girl was commenting about her. Was her dress gaudy, out of fashion, or somehow unbecoming?

Using the pet name he hadn't used since before her mother's death, Hamilton said, "Well Dolly, here we are. My little girl is all grown up."

"Father, I hope you won't address me so during our interview."

"Don't worry, I won't reveal your secret."

Hamilton was already climbing the first steps when Almira asked, "Do I look alright?"

"Yes, of course. You look very nice," he said.

"You're quite sure?"

"Yes, of course I'm sure. You look exactly like your mother when we were newly married. Does that answer you?"

Almira nodded.

"Take my arm and come with me."

Reaching the portico, Almira craned her neck upward. On either side of the doors stood banks of windows extending from the ground level through the entire four stories.

Though the day had already grown warm, the Hamiltons found the building cool inside. With the door closed, the continuous street noise of carriages and hooves on cobblestone vanished, replaced by a ticking clock. Someone was practicing piano. Feminine voices murmured above.

Almira followed her father up a wide staircase to the second floor. In the office two ladies sat at a large table. One of them looked very young, Almira thought at most fourteen. She was addressing envelopes. Another older, adult woman wearing black sleeve protectors looked up from a large bound book in which she was entering notations.

"Good morning. May I help you?" she asked.

"Yes, I am Mr. George Hamilton, of Willsborough. My daughter and I have an appointment this day with your principal."

"Very well," the receptionist said, "I will inform him you are here."

Principal Crittenton was an amiable and businesslike man of late middle age who met them with handshakes at the doorway of his office. "Please, take a seat and be comfortable," he said as he returned to his desk.

Crittenton went straight to the matter at hand. "From your letter, sir, I see that you wish to enroll your daughter Almira at our academy."

"That is correct. I have frequent business in Albany and have made inquiries into your institution's reputation. My wife is herself a graduate, class of 1828. We think this may be a fine place for my daughter to complete her education, and from which to take her place in society."

"I see," mused Crittenton. "I take it you are aware of our intentions here at this institution. Allow me, however, to reiterate them for you and your daughter so that we all understand each other fully. We strive to ensure that a diploma from the Albany Female Academy is regarded with the utmost respect. We do, of course, pay ample attention to the development of moral Christian sensibilities which are so essential to the character of any young lady of merit."

Almira could tell her father was already growing impatient with the principal's endless discourse.

"We also give attention to the social graces."

Almira imagined classes devoted to how one entertains well-mannered guests, maybe instructions in the piano forte, or painting with watercolors. Lessons presided over by a dance-master.

Her reverie was interrupted by Crittenton's lengthy description. "Our diploma is not awarded for mere attendance at class. No, all who pass through our course of study will emerge well acquainted with literature, mathematics, philosophy, and the natural sciences."

The principal looked at Almira, then at her father. He put on a pair of spectacles, picked up a letter that Hamilton had sent a month earlier, and scanned it. Returning his attention to Almira. "Now, it is my understanding that you have been tutored in French this last year?"

"*Oui monsieur*," Almira said.

The impetuous attempt to impress him forced Crittenton to smile, as much as he was trying to be stern. "We do offer lessons in French," he said, "if your father is willing to bear the additional expense, you can be enrolled with our professor of the Gallic tongue."

"If you mean French," interjected Hamilton, "that would be good. Speaking French is important for girls."

Crittenton reminded them that the academy wasn't a finishing school, then outlined the policies and conditions of boarding scholars. "I assure you that all are clean, Christian homes in which no pernicious influence is tolerated and regular attendance at church is expected."

This last point had never been important to Hamilton, but Almira's comfort and safety were. "Mail," he said. "What is the policy surrounding correspondence?"

"As her parent, you will provide a list of approved persons from whom your daughter may receive correspondence. No others will be delivered without your consent."

Gaining her father's permission to correspond with Sarah wouldn't be a problem, but letters from Daniel might be.

"Tell me, Miss Hamilton," Crittenton asked. "What are your finest features of character?"

Almira never anticipated a question like this. She sat silent for less than a minute, though it seemed much longer. She wanted to give an answer that at least showed her to be in possession of potential, if unrealized, brilliance. "I do have very fine equestrian skills."

After an awkward silence, Principal Crittenton said, "Do not fret, my dear girl. When you have completed your courses of study here, you will be able to articulate yourself with confidence. That is our mission, is it not?"

Almira nodded. Her father looked on proudly.

"Trusting that you have found our institution satisfactory, I hope to see you return." Crittenton turned to her Father. "Mr. Hamilton, please ask Miss Meigs to give you a tour of our building before you take your leave. We hope to see your daughter join us in September, and if that be the case, you may contact me with the necessary arrangement at this office."

Afterwards, while Almira and Hamilton waited for the cabbie to return, she said to him, "I made a grand fool of myself in there, I know I did."

"Dolly," he told her, "You will find in this life that it is not so much whether or not we play the fool, but whether we can pay the tuition."

Chapter 21

June, 1971

The luminous dial of the watch sitting beside the bed showed two-thirty a.m. Roused from his sleep, David knew right away why he was awake. Pulling on clothes, he snatched up his legal pad and pen as he left for the quiet room.

Almira stood at the north-facing window, peering out into the dark of night. "Hello, doctor." She smiled over her shoulder. "I thought you might be by to visit with me."

She'd been waiting for him? Why tonight? *Of course, that's it. Angela's gone. Almira must sense when she's here.* Her return, now that they were alone together again in the house, was no coincidence.

Then another idea hit. Was it possible Almira perceived Angela as competition, a rival for his attention? He'd never considered that before and, from a clinical point of view, the thought had intriguing therapeutic implications.

There was another dynamic here. Could Almira be a little jealous of Angela? David had to admit the idea was arousing. If she reciprocated his attraction, it seemed possible they could have a personal, even intimate relationship.

Almira and Angela. How would they react if they met face to face? Would Angela scream and run away? Would Almira vanish? Could the three of them hold a conversation together in the quiet room?

This last idea didn't have much appeal. In fact, David liked keeping the two relationships separate. Yes, Angela satisfied his need for sex, and she was a superb intellectual raconteur. She was companionable and her domesticity was comforting, but she also challenged him more than he liked.

Meanwhile, sessions with Miss Hamilton, separated as she was from all corruptions of the contemporary world, ensured he had her exclusive attention throughout the night. It was becoming an emotional necessity beyond his ability to resist.

Observing her turn from the window and slow approach toward him from across the room mesmerized him. This night, Almira wore a plaid dress with the very same black embroidered apron he'd seen before in her trunk. It was garish, but apparently not for her tastes.

Almira took a seat on her daybed, where she picked up a book resting upon it. Her every gesture, the way she moved through space, each succeeding posture she adopted, was studied and poised in a way no contemporary woman would ever conceive of. Her every move delighted him.

"This book recounts all the tales of Classical antiquity."

"Like the myth of Perseus and Andromeda?" he suggested.

"Yes, that in particular."

This was an opportunity to sound out her comprehension of elapsed time. "Do you remember the first time we met? That night you told me about how much you liked that story. Didn't you say you'd read it a thousand times?"

Almira knitted her brow and considered his question. "I do remember that. It has been, I think, a long, long time since."

"Less than a year, actually."

"Is that all," she said in wonderment. "Are you quite sure?"

"I am, but what I would like to know is, what in that myth appeals to you?"

"Is it any wonder I should be enamored of it? It's such a romantic story. Despite the chains that hold Andromeda captive, she is saved by the love of a strong and worthy man."

"Sometimes," David said, "when we read stories, we can imagine ourselves as one of the characters. Do you ever feel that way?"

"I do. I can imagine myself always. This is why I so love to read."

"In the myth of Andromeda and Perseus," he probed, "who would

150

you be?"

"Andromeda, of course."

"Are you held captive? Do you hope to be saved?"

"Perhaps," Almira said, each syllable pronounced as if it were a word in itself.

David let the silence hang between them, an invitation for her to expand this idea, but Almira said nothing. "All right." He decided it best to prompt her again. "If you see yourself as Andromeda, then who is Perseus?"

"Daniel," she said.

She comprehends the psychological symbolism, thought David. Hoping to continue the conversation's momentum, he pressed further. "And who is Cassiopeia?"

Almira thought about this question for a full minute before she answered. "That would be my father. His pride thinks me above the love of a good man."

David commented that this was a sophisticated interpretation of the classical myth, and though Almira agreed it might be, she still declined to explore the analysis further. He supposed she needed time to become comfortable with the idea. He wouldn't press the point further for now. David jotted a note to return to the subject again another time.

"Do you not think all women are held captive in some way?" Almira said.

David looked up from his legal pad and raised an eyebrow. "Is that so?"

"Yes, we are. By the expectations of others and by our own impulsive nature."

"Is that what this story is about?" he asked. "How we must be freed from the consequences of our own impulses?"

At first, Almira didn't answer. She smoothed the apron on her lap. "Don't we all struggle with our impulses at times? I should think we do. Life is a battle of wills. Sometimes the battle is lost. Then we must atone for our foolish acts or be forced to defend them forever."

She got up from her divan and walked back to the window.

"Are you looking for something out there?" asked David.

Almira twisted around and pressed a finger to her lips. Returning to the daybed, she leaned in and whispered, "If I confide something to you, you must promise not to tell."

"Of course."

"I am waiting for a sign that Daniel has returned," she whispered.

The next morning David planted the "Open" sign at the end of the drive, opened the doors of the carriage house wide and waited for business. He busied himself with refinishing an Eastlake armoire. Someone had painted it pink years ago, ruined it really, but restoring things was a worthwhile activity.

Though his hands were busy, his mind remained preoccupied by Almira's recent remarks about the consequences of impulsivity.

A station wagon ground to a stop in the drive and its passengers got out. David wiped his hands, more annoyed at the interruption than happy to see potential customers. He eyed them, recognizing the type. They probably hailed from Westchester county or New Jersey, too affluent for their own good.

The husband, David assumed, arched his back and groaned. His Bermuda shorts, glaring white legs, and sandals with dark socks identified him as a business-suit, corporate type. Commercial real estate or a lawyer maybe. The wife had permed hair and wore huge sunglasses and artificially worn jeans with expensive shoes.

A boy about four years old tumbled out through the tailgate, jittering and grabbing his crotch through stiff dungarees, rolled half-way to his knees.

The wife walked up to David, pulling the boy with her. "Do you have a restroom for my son?"

"Huh, I guess, sure." He pointed to the house. "Go through the screen door. First room on the left."

"Joey, come with mommy."

She extended her jewelry-covered hand and long, blood-red nails. *What would she be like between the sheets*, David wondered. *Those nails look like dangerous weapons.*

"She's redecorating," the husband said. "Last year it was Italian provincial. Now she wants everything colonial."

"Sure, it's popular."

The husband looked around. "What's this place zoned?" he asked. "You know, if you've got a few acres, you could subdivide it, put up a development. Sell it as lakefront property. I know some builders."

David ignored the suggestion.

"How old is this place anyway? It looks like *Gone With The Wind.*"

"About three-hundred-and-fifty-years old," David said. The lie felt good. It drew more of a distinction between them.

The wife returned with the kid, who ran through the shop, handling things he didn't understand.

"Do you have any milk cans?" she asked.

"Milk cans?"

"You know, like the cows use. They're metal with big handles."

"She wants me to paint them flat black and put decals all over them. Eagles, and shit like that."

"Norm, honey, it's colonial."

David sent them up the road to Gary's dairy farm. His neighbor had dozens of them stacked in his milking barn, obsolete and rusting. He'd be thrilled to get a few of them off his hands for quick cash.

As the station wagon doors slammed shut, David thought that selling retail antiques to tourists was another failed idea. At least doing psychotherapy, he had predictable appointments, more control, and less intrusion. No, it wasn't what you'd call an auspicious start to Carriage House Antiques.

David closed the doors to the shop and went back into the house. He wiped off the toilet seat and fixtures with Lysol, then poured a shot of Slivovitz and knocked it back.

Upstairs in the quiet room he opened the trunk, retrieved Almira's daguerreotype, and brought it down to a work area he used to clean and examine small antiques.

Perched on a metal stool, David opened the case again, but this time he viewed the image under a strong, lighted magnifier affixed to a flexible neck. Daguerreotypes had always fascinated him. Their infinite layers of detail seemed more a gateway to the living past than a frozen reflection of it. The brass matte felt like a portal and, whenever David looked closely at a daguerreotype, he always had the urge to step through it and into the world beyond.

He inserted the blade of a utility knife between the glass that covered the daguerreotype and the case in which it was held. Using sideways pressure, he lifted the glass, brass matte and the copper plate as one unit. As was the usual practice, they had been sealed together with glued tape at the gallery where the plate was processed. Much of the tape had dried and no longer adhered. David scraped the residue from the glass and copper plate, allowing him to pull them apart. He placed the glass and brass matte to one side. With the entire plate visible it revealed more of Almira's dress and the edge of what he guessed to be light-reflecting panels on either side. The wider view presented her as less isolated, suggesting as it did the surroundings of a studio with photographic apparatus.

David noticed impressions in one corner of the silver-coated plate, a stamp reading "WM. H. BUTLER N-YORK."

He was pretty sure this meant the photographer had purchased the copper plates already silver coated and thus hallmarked to indicate source and purity. He was in the habit of checking these hallmarks against those already catalogued to help identify and date finer metal antiques, but there was no match in his reference books for this one.

A photographic copy stand was set up nearby. David loaded a roll of film into his Pentax camera, screwed on a macro lens, attached a cable release, then mounted it to the stand. With the daguerreotype under the lens, David looked through the viewfinder. He made a few adjustments and took two dozen exposures.

Before reassembling the daguerreotype, he wanted to look over Almira's portrait once more—this time with a jeweler's loupe. He could discern the ivory tip of the drawn parasol she held in her lap, the darts in her bodice behind the lace of her pelisse, the diagonal sweep of her clavicle bones and the slope of her bare shoulders, and what looked like the same coral necklace she wore during their sessions.

Bringing the focus to her eyes, an idea came… If he was looking into the past, wasn't she staring into the future? And wasn't the camera itself reflected in her pupils? Was that even possible? Of course, it was—this was a daguerreotype. Daguerreotypes had the power to evoke questions like these.

David decided against placing Almira's portrait back inside the trunk. Her image was too perfect, too beautiful in subject, composition and execution to lock away out of sight

Chapter 22

Late Summer, 1841

The need to be alone with Daniel, to tell him about the trip to Albany was overwhelming, but Almira had to wait nearly a week before the right time presented itself. That Saturday, her father left to be gone all day to Willsborough Falls. Loretta sat in the parlor, reading and sipping sherry. Almira entered and announced. "I have a riding lesson with Daniel at noon."

Loretta's glib reply, showing more interest in the magazine than her, relieved Almira. Her initiative might have been seen as brazen. After all, she and Daniel would be unchaperoned. As it was, Almira didn't need to employ her rehearsed excuses—that she was nearly nineteen, old enough to make such a decision for herself. Since Saturday afternoons were customarily the hired men's own time, Daniel wouldn't be neglecting his work on the property.

From where she waited at the mounting stone, she watched Daniel bring their horses from the carriage house. So handsome was he, she could easily imagine him in the dashing uniform of a British lancer.

Eager to be alone, Almira and Daniel rode toward the lake with little conversation until, safely out of sight, they halted their horses. Almira's heart beat wildly as she enjoyed their lingering kiss from the saddle.

"God," Daniel said as their lips parted. "My darling girl, how I've missed you."

"And I you, Danny. I thought of you constantly."

"Come, let's ride for a while."

On the way, Almira started to tell Daniel about the way she'd informed her stepmother of their intentions to ride together that afternoon.

"I hope it doesn't cause a ruckus," he said. "You know, Mirie, sooner or later I'll have to be honest with your father about us. Things can't go on this way."

Almira tossed it off. "Let's not think about it now."

They rode for a long time that afternoon. Along the way Almira described the Empress, the Rawsons and the sentimental Scotsman. She described Albany and the Albion hotel. But when she spoke about the Albany Female Academy, she noticed a shadow cast itself across Daniel's face.

"Don't be sad, Danny," she said. "I must go, but I'll be gone only a few months. I'll ask Father to allow me to receive letters from you. It could be romantic to be each other's correspondents. Don't you think so?"

He didn't. Eventually they found themselves dismounting at their usual, private place, the knoll overlooking the lake. The sun had taken on the hint of late summer's glow, and early crickets chirped from the trees around them.

"I've brought something special with me. I expect you'll find it very interesting." She pulled the daguerreotype from her dress pocket and held it out. "Go ahead. Take it. Undo the cover. I think you'll like what you find inside."

Daniel opened it. Seeing his face light up thrilled her.

"It's a daguerreotype, isn't it?" He stammered. "It's a daguerreotype of you."

"Yes, Father had it done while we were in Albany. He keeps it on his desk. He doesn't know I took it, but I knew you'd want to see it."

Daniel looked at her, then at the daguerreotype, then at her again. He held it at a variety of angles, expressed fascination at the way it would shift from a positive to a negative image. The way it took on the reflectivity of a mirror.

"Here," she said. "I'll use my straw to shade it."

Daniel asked Almira to describe the entire process. How long did it take? Who was the artist? What did the camera look like? Finally, he asked, "Do you think it's something I could do?"

"Yes, I can't imagine why not. There is the camera box and some bad-smelling chemicals, but other than those things, it seemed easily done."

"I've been reading more about daguerreotypes in the newspapers. Did you know I cut out the articles and keep them? The biggest cities have studios, but most towns still don't." He absently rubbed his cleft chin. Almira could sense his mind racing.

"Mirie, I know there'll be a lot of business opportunities. If I became a daguerreotypist, I wouldn't be a common laborer anymore. I could support you properly. I'd be a professional and a businessman, which is something your father might respect." Daniel stood up, offering his hand. As tall as he was, and loving him as she did, it felt perfect to look up and take it. "Speaking of daguerreotypes, we'd better get back. We need to return this to your father's desk before he finds it missing."

A coolness rose from the lake as they rode at a brisk trot in the safest places. Daniel praised Almira's skill with Ginger Snap, which pleased her very much.

"As I've advised you many times, it is a matter of control. If you are frightened, the horse can tell. The principle is really quite simple."

Daniel laughed at her teasing instructions. So did she.

"The Odd Fellows Hall in Willsborough Falls is having a picnic next Sunday," he said. "Wouldn't it be nice if we could go together?"

"Really? I'd love that. I haven't picnicked since before Mother became ill. Will there be dancing?" she asked.

"Oh, bless me, yes, there'll be fiddlers and dancing aplenty."

The idea of dancing to a fiddler thrilled Almira. She wondered aloud at the fun they might have, even as they rode past the clothesline where, out of sight, Julia and Sally hung sheets to dry.

After being summoned to Hamilton's office, Daniel stood before him, cap in hand.

"Then you admit you have been repeatedly taking Almira riding, alone, without chaperone and without asking my or my wife's permission."

"Yes, Mr. Hamilton," said Daniel. "But please, it's nothing we haven't done since last summer when you asked me to teach her."

"Quiet," Hamilton said, his tone more of a bark. "I've also discovered that you intend to take my daughter to a common tradesmen's gathering. Just how did you presume to do any such thing without my expressed consent?"

Daniel tried to answer. "Sir, me and Miss Almira, it was an innocent thing."

"I'm not interested in innocent things."

"Please sir, let me—"

"Silence!" Hamilton drummed his fingers on his desk, the same desk where Almira's miniature was displayed, as if she were present in the room with them. "Daniel, you've betrayed me. I took you in, gave you a job and a place to sleep when you had nothing. I was more of a father to you than you've ever known. And how do you repay me? With this? Leading my daughter into these secret assignations?"

"But, sir, if you knew how much I love Almira."

Hamilton rose to his full height and pressed his knuckles into the top of his desk. "Love? Love? You stupid boy, what do you know of love? Love means you have something to offer. You have nothing, nothing at all. A horse might as well tell me he loves my daughter."

Daniel felt a surge of anger. His complexion turned red. "Don't call me a horse. I'm not a horse. I'm much more than a horse."

The clock ticked. Hamilton fumed.

"Yes, I suppose you are," the gentleman admitted, his ire momentarily checked. "But neither are you of a class with Almira. She's not one of your common lakeshore girls of the type you would be acquainted with, do you understand me?"

"Mr. Hamilton, sir, I never—"

"Be quiet." Hamilton stormed. "And mark my words, if I find out that you have so much as laid a finger upon Almira, I'll have you charged with an outrage against her person."

Daniel clenched his teeth in rage, his jaw set. The suggestion that the love he and Almira shared was something disgraceful gave him the urge to give his patron a good thrashing.

"Listen carefully, young man. You are dismissed from my employ as of this instant. Gather up your things from the carriage house and be gone. Any books of mine you have you may leave with Julia. Sandborne will deliver you whatever wages you have coming. And so help me God, if I ever, ever hear of you coming near my daughter again there will be the devil to pay. Do I make myself clear?"

"Yes sir, very clear."

As he stepped into the hallway Daniel looked up to see Almira kneeling at the top of the stairs, dissolving into tears. She'd heard everything. He knew it.

"Danny, Danny no. Don't go."

Daniel raised a finger to his lips and mouthed the words, "I'll come back for you." Then he turned and walked out.

Almira rose. She wanted to run after him, but it was too late. Hamilton had stepped from his office to block her way.

"Go to your rooms," he ordered.

Within the privacy of her sitting room, Almira's mind raced. What her father had done was so unjust. He had insinuated shameful things about her and Daniel's love. No, their love was pure—which could hardly be said for him and that drunken interloper from Plattsburgh.

Almira looked at a pink luster teacup on her writing table. It was delicate and pretty, but something about its effete beauty ignited her rage. She hurled the cup into the fireplace. It exploded into shards against the stone masonry, as broken as her heart.

A half hour passed. Sally tapped on her door.

"Miss, your father wants to see you."

Almira composed herself and descended the stairs. At the door she knocked lightly.

"Come in," he said.

Almira entered. Her father was slouched at his desk, pinching the bridge of his nose. Except for the clock ticking, the room was altogether silent. "Almira, sit down. I suppose you know why I want to speak to you."

"Yes, Father," she said, as she took a chair.

"Is there anything I should know? Anything of a sensitive nature?" he asked.

"No," she said. "I am still...innocent...still intact." Her bold answer stopped short of defiance.

"Thank God." He exhaled with relief. "Almira, do you understand why this liaison is so improper?"

"I know why you think so, but you're wrong."

"Wrong that I want the best for you?" he asked. "You are a young lady of some background. Daniel is an Irish papist of low breeding.

He's entirely unsuited for a girl such as yourself."

"Mother was very fond of him," Almira countered. "She encouraged us to be together. If she were here now, she would tell you this herself."

"I seriously doubt that." He sneered. "No, if your mother were here, she would agree that this infatuation offends the rules of propriety."

Flooded by anger, Almira knew that what she was about to say would be explosive but felt justified. "Really? Offensive to propriety? I should think the time for propriety is long since passed, at least in this household."

From his reaction, Almira could tell her father was unprepared and taken aback by what she'd said. It emboldened her, so she spoke again. "Do you not think that your haste to remarry has been an embarrassment to our family? I, for one, should like to know the extent of your friendship with Loretta before Mother died."

"How dare you insinuate such a thing," he shouted, half standing from his chair and sputtering with rage. "You impudent girl. You're in no position to discuss secret liaisons of any kind." Hamilton charged ahead. "Do you not see—he has nothing to offer for your hand?"

Almira stood her ground. "You had nothing when you met Mother."

"My God, you dare make a comparison between me and that boy?" Hamilton's rage was in full force. "You, you who are accustomed to the best of everything. You who have not yet had the decency to visit your mother's grave."

The words stung and Almira could not hide it. Hamilton kept up the offensive.

"Just what do you think that dirty stable boy will ever bring you? He has no future."

"He does. Danny's going to become a Daguerreian artist."

"A what?"

"A Daguerreian artist," she repeated.

Hamilton slammed his fist on the desk. "Enough of this nonsense. I forbid you to see him or have any communication. In two weeks you leave for Albany. You'll forget about Daniel. You'll meet suitable young men, and this will all be a schoolgirl's folly. Now go to your room and say no more about this."

She remained seated. Her jaw was set, her face red, eyes dark with anger.

"Are you deaf? Did you not hear me?"

160

Almira stood without taking her eyes off her father's face, swiveled on her heel, stormed out and immediately collided with Julia and Sally eavesdropping at the door. "Get out of my way, you stupid girls." She pushed past them and ran up the stairs.

Back in her chambers, Almira took a seat by the window. From this position she could observe the carriage house and part of the barn behind it. Heartbroken at being separated from her beloved, and hopeless for her future, she thought of running away with Daniel. She took out a sheet of paper and her inkwell to write a farewell letter to her father, but the fantasy was so outlandish, it collapsed under the weight of another gush of tears.

As she tore up the paper, Almira saw Daniel emerge from the carriage house, leading Marcus by the reins. He was within calling distance, but anything she said would be overheard by her father, Loretta, or those busybody servant girls. Even at this distance, she saw how wounded his expression was whenever he cast his eyes toward her.

With Marcus hitched to the railing, Daniel brought out a carpet bag, an overcoat and a fowling piece, and secured them to the saddle.

Lastly, he brought out a short stack of books. Julia met him halfway across the yard and took them. He returned to Marcus and cinched up the leather harness and straps, securing all his possessions. Taking his horse by the reins, the young man looked around at the one home he'd ever known, turned to the one girl he'd ever loved, and waved goodbye.

Almira leaned far out of the window and, shielding her eyes, watched him disappear up the road.

The mood at the breakfast table was tense. Hamilton projected irritation, Almira remained silent, and Loretta looked like someone caught between two snarling dogs. Desperate to mediate, she asked if Almira wasn't excited to be attending the Albany Female Academy.

"I shall be pleased to be among enlightened society," she said.

"I'm sure you will, my dear," said Loretta. "I should say that my three years there were among the happiest of my life, and certainly the most stimulating."

These stilted exchanges with her stepmother were the limit of the conversation. Hamilton confined his attention to his newspaper and coffee.

Finally, as he rose from the table, Almira spoke to him. "Father, I

161

should like to take Ginger Snap riding this day. May I ask Sandborne to saddle her?"

Hamilton grunted his permission and left. A minute later, Almira rose too. "Thank you. If I may be excused, I now have my French compositions to study."

Later that afternoon Almira waited at the mounting stone for Sandborne to bring her pony.

"You'll be quite all right, miss, riding by yourself?" he asked, as he positioned Ginger Snap for her to mount. "If you wish I can ride alongside."

"That is kind of you, Sandborne, but I need some time alone. Don't worry, I'll exercise caution."

"Very well, miss, I understand. When you return you may leave her in the paddock. I'll see to it she's combed and put away."

Almira rode off slowly, in truth a little nervous about riding by herself. Every other time she'd ridden, she'd been with Daniel. His advice sounded in her mind. "Remember, Ginger Snap is a gentle horse. She wants to be ridden gently."

She could see how right he was. Ginger Snap ambled along at a relaxed, unhurried pace, reflexively taking her to the rise overlooking the lake.

A good daughter would visit her mother's grave, Almira thought. *It was only a few rods away, after all, nestled in those trees.* She stared at the pathway leading through the grove, but the expected sting of rebuke was too strong to dare enter.

Instead she dismounted and settled alone with her broken heart, where she and Daniel had sat so many times together. Almira gazed out on the landscape. Afternoon sunlight bathed the countryside. Trees along the mountain ridges were still a deep green, the lake a deep blue. She could see red and white farm buildings scattered among the Vermont hills. A schooner with its sails full of the southern breeze was making its majestic way to Plattsburgh. Exciting as Albany was, she thought, this was where she belonged. It would be hard for her to ever leave this place.

From far across a neighboring field, Sandborne watched. He'd been trailing her from a distance since she rode away from the house, partly out of concern and partly to find an opportunity to speak with her privately.

Seeing her dismounted, he hobbled along painfully, for his leg had been giving him much trouble in recent weeks, along fence rows and hedges, followed by his old dog until he came near. She sat on a rock ledge, looking out toward the lake, where he'd seen her and Daniel before.

"Miss Almira," he called.

She turned and hastily wiped the tears from her eyes.

"I'm sorry, miss," he said. "I don't wish to disturb you in your sadness, but may I sit here beside you?"

Almira nodded. The old man winced as he took a seat with her on the ledge.

"I spoke with Daniel yesterday before he left."

"What did he say? Please Mr. Sandborne, tell me everything."

"He wants you to know that he will wait for you until the day you and he can be together."

"Oh," said Almira with a little yelp. "Thank goodness."

"There is more. Daniel told me he would leave letters for you at the post office in my name."

"But how can I receive them without my father knowing?"

Sandborne had already considered the question. "Listen carefully. There is a cracked molasses crock on my workbench in the carriage house. I keep tools in it. When one of his letters arrives, I will hide it in there. You will know it is there by a taper I will light in the carriage house window."

"And if I wish to send a message to Daniel, I should do the same?"

"Yes, you will light a taper in the window of your sitting room. I will see it and know to fetch your letter from the crock."

"Did he say any more?"

"Only that you oughtn't to worry, and that he loved you beyond all else."

Almira squeezed Sandborne's forearm. He patted her hand.

"I know it seems you and Danny are in a peck of trouble," he said. "But everything will be alright. Trust in the Lord and you'll see."

"You're right. It's just I love Daniel so, and we want only to be together."

The old gentleman stood up and tipped his hat. "I must go now. Do you need help with your horse, miss?"

"No Sandborne, thank you. I can mount her easily from this ledge, or I might even walk her back."

"Whichever is your pleasure, please do be careful, miss," he said. "I mean about everything." Sandborne touched his hat again and limped away.

Chapter 23

June 25, 1971

It was late but long-distance charges were a lot cheaper after eleven p.m. David sat on the porch steps off the kitchen door with the telephone cord stretched as far as it would go. Uncomfortable, yes, but the solitude, the stars, and the chirping of crickets made it worthwhile.

"You know what," said Angela, her voice breathy through the receiver. "My roommate Tina was telling me she spent last weekend at Shelter Island. She said it was a real scream."

"Shelter Island—that's way the hell out on the eastern end of Long Island."

"Yeah, I guess it's out in the Hamptons or something."

A sound hollow and metallic came through the other end. David guessed she was sipping from a can of beer.

"We ought to check it out," she said. "C'mon, we'll have a weekend beach party for two."

David couldn't disagree, there were some really nice beaches in the Hamptons. "And those are some old places out there. Not just Shelter Island. Gardiner's Island, Sag Harbor. I think there's a museum about the whaling industry. Would you mind if we went there?"

"Jesus, David. You and your museums."

Though he couldn't see it, he knew she was rolling her eyes.

"Hey," she said. "Didn't you once tell me a joke about being reincarnated as a whale?"

"I forgot about that one. It's kind of dirty. I must have been pretty loaded if I told you that one."

"You were," said Angela, trying to stifle a belch. "It was on the night we met."

"Oh my God." He laughed. "That's right."

Angela returned to the subject at hand. "So, what about that idea? Shelter Island. We can go to your whale museum first and spend the rest of the time lying on the beach and, you know, fooling around."

The idea sounded nice and yet he still hesitated.

"Baby," she said, trying again. "It would be really nice. Fourth of July weekend is tough for me."

"What do you mean?"

"My mother died on the Fourth, so it kind of spoils the holiday for me."

"You never told me about that."

"No, I don't talk about it."

David sensed there was more but said nothing, letting silence do the work. The sound of an empty can tossed into the trash rattled through the receiver.

"I was sixteen, almost seventeen," she said. "My kid brother was twelve. He took it pretty hard."

"What about you?" he asked. "It had to have been tough for you too."

David heard the refrigerator door open and close.

"For a couple of days, yeah. After that, not so much. I was too busy being pissed off."

"What happened to her?" he asked.

"She had lung cancer."

The noise of a kitchen drawer being yanked open, then bumped closed with a hip, was followed by the distinctive pop and fizz of a can opener piercing metal.

"It spread everywhere," she said, between long swallows. "The last few weeks, she was pretty out of it. They had her all doped up. I couldn't take it. Most of the time I stayed away."

"It sounds horrible."

"Yeah, it was pretty bad. Toward the end, I couldn't even stand to look at her. She just wanted me to stay and hold her hand and tell me she loved me. It was unbearable."

"I'm sorry. I didn't know."

"Well it's not something I talk about." Angela took another drink. He heard the metallic sound of the can coming down hard on the table. "Anyway, it's done and over. After that, I did a lot of stupid shit for a few years. What did the school psychologist call it? Oh yeah, acting out. Did I say that right?"

"That all depends on what it was," said David.

"Sexual stuff."

He'd asked this in a clinical sense, but Angela's frank answer was disarming. David didn't know how to respond.

"Yeah." She belched again. "I was pretty popular for a while, but I'm a one-man woman now."

"What were you so pissed off about?"

"A lot of things, I guess. I was mad that my mother was dead, not that it was her fault. Mad at my dad too."

"Why were you so put off with him?"

"My old man? He's a typical guy. I found out later he was getting it on with his secretary the whole time my mother was dying."

"That's rough," said David. "Are you still angry with him?"

"Not really. My mom was sick for a long time. He was lonely and men are animals anyway." Angela finished her beer and sighed. "Look, it was a bad time for everybody, including him. He got remarried—not to his secretary, but to someone else."

"Do you like her?"

"She's okay, and now she and my father are expecting a kid of their own, so he's got a completely new family. He'll be a father again at fifty-five."

"Life's strange, isn't it?"

"You can say that again."

It sounded to him like she needed to get these experiences off her chest—what one of his patients used to call a "brain vomit", so he let her go on. "Like I was saying, it was my brother who took it the worst. It really effed him up. He's been a basket case ever since."

A famous experiment designed to test attachment theory popped into David's mind. A psychologist, Harry Harlow, forced baby monkeys to choose between two dummy mothers—one of which gave milk but was cold and hard, and another which gave no nourishment but was warm and soft. Preferring to feel an imitation of love even if it meant gnawing hunger, most of the baby monkeys clung to the soft one and starved to death. Those few survivors were, like Angela had said, really effed up. He'd heard Harlow was a real bastard.

The receiver on the other end sounded like it shifted again. And now she sounded like she spoke with a cigarette in her mouth. David could visualize it easily. She'd have that huge purse on her lap, fumbling around in it for a book of matches. He'd seen her do it many times.

"I feel bad for him," she said, as she struck a match, took a drag, and exhaled. "He's like a lost soul, my brother. He goes from one dead end job to another. If he's not careful he's going to get sent to Viet Nam."

"Don't worry, we're almost out of there."

"Oh, sure we are."

David ignored her sarcasm, heard the sequence of refrigerator door, opener piercing metal, Angela gulping suds. This had become a heavy conversation. He tried to shift gears. "Where's your roommate tonight?"

"Tina? She's on an overnight to London. She won't be back until tomorrow." Angela swallowed. "Maybe I should have become a stewardess. The uniform would turn you on, wouldn't it?"

"Well, sure, yeah."

An owl hooted from the direction of the carriage house. Angela had gone quiet, so David resumed the conversation. "I don't think Tina likes me very much."

"Oh, Tina's okay. Don't let her bother you. She's supercilious, but that's just the way she is."

He heard the thunk of another can being tossed in the trash.

"You should be impressed," she said. "For a girl who just had four beers, I'd say I pronounced that pretty good."

"You mean, pretty well, but yes, I'd have to agree."

"So, what do you think? About Shelter Island?"

"Well, it would be hard for me to get away for that long. It's a haul down there to the city and then way out to the Hamptons."

"Wah, wah," she chided. "You're getting to be like a grumpy old man. Is poor David's arthritis acting up again?"

"Okay. Next weekend might work. I can come down on Thursday night. There's a few things I need to check on in the city, but even if we leave Saturday morning, we can be out there in two or three hours."

"Super. I'll be packed and ready."

"You know, there's another museum I've wanted to go to for a long time. It's in Stony Brook. They have an exhibit of paintings by William

Sidney Mount."

She wasn't familiar with Mount—not many people were—so he filled her in on the basic facts. "See, Mount was this nineteenth century genre painter from Long Island. He painted everyday people doing everyday things. He's kind of known for being the first guy to portray black people as real people, on an equal par with whites."

Angela pointed out that Tina's weekend didn't include visits to art museums. "But why not, baby, if it makes you happy?"

"You're a doll. How about I meet you Thursday when you get off work? In the meantime, we better close this out. These long-distance charges are murder."

"I know, but, David, before we hang up, I want to say thanks for listening to me. Usually I don't say anything about all this stuff, but it's been really good talking with you."

"My pleasure," he said. "Honest, I mean it. It's nice to get to know you better."

Angela exhaled, a long purr from the receiver, low and intimate. "You know, baby. Sometimes you seem so far away all the way up there. But not tonight. Tonight I feel really close to you."

David hadn't been off the phone for long when reasons this Shelter Island idea wouldn't work started eating at him. For one thing, the big antiques fair at Brimfield was the following weekend. It's the world-series of antiques. You don't just throw some crap in a U-Haul trailer and go. No, everything had to be planned, inventoried, and carefully selected for maximum effect. All those things took time and David didn't like to be rushed.

The bigger issue was one of geography. They'd be driving the length of Long Island, from Brooklyn to Montauk Point, which meant they'd pass within a few miles of Angela's parents in Smithtown. Even if he made it plain he had no interest in visiting, he could see it already. They'd be tired, or she would be, anyway. She'd suggest they stop in just for five minutes, just long enough to meet them. *Before you know it, we're staying for dinner, spending the night, and running a day behind schedule.*

Almira didn't make these kinds of demands of him. She didn't ask him to do things he was reluctant to do. She stayed in the Quiet Room. If he wanted her, she'd be there.

169

Chapter 24

August, 1841

All through the following week, Almira waited to see a candle burning in the carriage house window, but there were none. On Monday, Sandborne took the wagon to Elizabethtown and returned with a teen-aged boy. When Almira passed the old man near the orchard, he told her the boy's name was Jeremiah, the new hired hand.

"Have you seen him?" she asked quietly, taking care not to use Daniel's name.

"No," Sandborne whispered. "But someone's told me he's working on the steamboat *Burlington.*"

With her heart buoyed by the knowledge of where Daniel was, Almira made a point over the following days to walk or ride to their private place overlooking Lake Champlain as often as she could, hoping to catch a glimpse of him if the vessel should pass.

Waiting at the ledge one afternoon, her mind wandered back to the day she'd first set eyes on him. How old had she been, fifteen? She remembered peering at him from the kitchen doorway. So thin and ragged, Mother had fed him and dressed his burns. Father gave him two old shirts.

In those days, Daniel followed her father and Sandborne around like a puppy, but in recent years he had grown into the strongest man in the household. Now Daniel was gone.

On the fifth day of standing watch, she was rewarded. A ship came down the lake belching smoke and churning up water. She read the name *Burlington* emblazoned in red and gold letters on the paddlewheel housing. She could see men on deck too, though it was impossible to recognize any one individual. Yet Daniel must be somewhere among them on board, and that meant he could possibly see her as well. Almira stood on the ledge. Though she jumped up and down waving her leghorn hat, in a few minutes the ship was too far to discern details any longer. She stopped. Standing still, she felt her heart beating as if it could fly off and be with him.

The time when she would leave for Albany came nearer. Almira inspected every article of her clothing—mending, altering, and replacing as necessary. It being nearly a year since her mother's death, and in the interest of fashion, the black decorations on her bonnet were taken off and the original plaid ribbons restored. Though Loretta supplied one of her own trunks to supplement Almira's cowhide valise, hard choices still had to be made regarding what to take and what to leave behind.

That evening, Hamilton commented at supper on mail just received. Sandborne must have been to the post office sometime that day. Would there be a lighted candle tonight? As soon as she could extricate herself from the meal Almira rushed upstairs with petticoats gathered in her fists.

Though twilight, waiting for nightfall had to be endured. Almira sat by the window until it was too dim to read, then she set her magazine aside and watched cat-like for a point of yellow light in the loft window.

And suddenly, there it was, Sandborne's signal burning like the fire in her heart—in Daniel's heart she hoped as well. Almira wanted to rush across the yard right then and scurry inside the carriage house to fetch her message, but Sandborne's warning to be careful repeated in her mind. It was too dangerous. In the end she resigned herself to wait until morning.

Most of the night she lay awake, restless, anticipating what the letter would say, remembering the quiet moments they'd spent together, and imagining what would happen if she could be again in his arms. She contemplated how her life had become like her favorite novels as she fell asleep.

It was broad daylight when Almira woke. From the sound of things, she'd missed breakfast. Sally, who was already upstairs and making the beds, offered to bring up a cup of tea. Seated on her daybed, Almira sipped tea and contemplated how she could get into the carriage house without being noticed.

With her toilet finished she went downstairs. Loretta was in the parlor, sitting on the sofa, reading and enjoying her morning concoction of gin with cream and nutmeg. Baby Dorothea lay asleep beside her.

"Good morning, my dear," her stepmother said.

Almira sat down. They talked about incidental things until Loretta made an invitation. "I intend this new boy Jeremiah to drive me and your father into the village this afternoon. Why don't you come along?"

"Thank you, but I didn't sleep well last night." Her glee was hard to conceal. "It would be better for me to rest, I think."

Perfect—as long as Julia didn't see her, it would be easy to retrieve her letter with her parents away. Indeed, the Hamiltons had only been gone a few moments when Almira set out to retrieve Daniel's letter.

Taking long steps, she strode across the yard to the carriage house. Hopefully the large basket on her elbow would make Julia and Sally think she had gone to pick vegetables or early apples.

At the carriage house she stopped, glanced over her shoulder, and stepped through the door. The inside was dim. Particles of dust floated through the single beam of sunlight streaming in through the window over Sandborne's workbench.

Waiting for her eyes to adjust, Almira was startled out of her skin by a cat's meow.

"Wigwam, no. Go away," she scolded, but he kept looking up at her innocently. She crouched, stroked the top of his head and pulled on his jowls. "Very well then," she whispered, "but you must promise to be quiet."

They walked through the interior together. Almira scanned the bench for the cracked molasses jar without success. Wigwam jumped up onto the surface of the bench and walked silently across the top. There it was, with various tools protruding, Wigwam rubbing his face across its rim. With heart pounding, she reached inside, feeling among the unfamiliar wrenches and screwdrivers, until she felt it—an envelope. Almira plucked it out. "Mr. Emmet Sandborne, Willsborough Falls, Essex County, New York" written across the front.

With the letter secured inside her dress pocket, Almira made her way to the orchard. She picked two dozen apples indiscriminately and returned to the house, where she discarded them in the kitchen and flew

173

up the back staircase to her sitting room.

Without bothering to sit down, she opened the envelope and unfolded the paper inside.

My Darling, you will forgive my not sending a letter sooner, but I have not had the opportunity to leave mail until now. I have only a moment to write this. Since I left, I have been working on the lake. It is a torment for me to be separated from you. I know you are soon to leave for Albany but someday we won't ever have to be apart again. There is much, much more I wish to say to you. Can you meet me in the orchard this Saturday at midnight? I will tell you more then.

I sign this with all my love.
Yours, D. Dwyer.

By Saturday afternoon Almira's excitement was hard to contain. When the clock in the parlor chimed twice, immediately joined by another in her father's office, she was disappointed. Minutes were dragging into long hours, and it would still be ten more before her meeting that night with Daniel.

First, she went to the parlor, but she found piano practice impossible with her concentration preoccupied. Returning upstairs, she wandered aimlessly between her bedroom and sitting room. She lounged on her daybed. She picked up a novel she'd been reading and finished it.

Almira took out a letter she'd received from Sarah Rawson the week before and read it once again, trying to visualize her friend's description of the falls and the newlywed's journey on the Erie Canal. According to Sarah, the packet boat from Waterford to Buffalo was larger than the *Empress*, with a chambermaid to attend to their comforts and a comic minstrel show to entertain the passengers.

She wanted to write Sarah a long letter in return, except that she'd already answered this one twice, and writing about the reasons for her current excitement was risky.

Instead, Almira sat before her dressing mirror. She tied up her hair in an Apollo knot, plucked her eyebrows, and buffed her nails. She unpacked her trunk and checked everything once more. As she repacked it again, the chimes announced that it was five o'clock. Was that all? What did Mother say about needlework? That its true purpose was to teach the control of one's impulses.

She took out her sewing basket. It would be of more interest to work on Daniel's braces, but that would be taking chances, so she put them away.

Wandering back to the kitchen she took an apple for herself and two more for Ginger Snap. Loretta and Sally were outside in the flower garden with Egbert, who came running toward her calling, "Mirra, Mirra."

She bent down as he came near and asked him, "Would you like to share my apple?"

Egbert nodded enthusiastically. He took a bite and smiled. He was, she had to admit, a dear little fellow. "Would you like to help Almira feed Ginger Snap a treat?" she asked as she put on her straw hat.

He placed a sticky hand in hers and they walked off toward the paddock.

"See how she comes to us?"

Ginger Snap nickered for the apple Almira held out with one hand while she petted her pony's forehead with the other.

"I will miss you, but Sandborne and Egbert will take good care of you until I return. Isn't that so, Egbert?"

He nodded and promised he would bring a treat every day. Almira instructed Egbert to hold the next apple by the stem and offer it to the pony. He giggled with delight when the animal took a big bite.

"Now hold the apple in the flat of your palm," she said. "Ginger will eat it from your hand."

The rest of the day went slowly. Supper was laden with tedious instructions. When her father snapped, "Did you hear me, child? These matters are important," she knew he'd lost his patience.

Almira retired early. She lay beneath her coverlet, but awake and dressed, counting the hours until Perseus would come for his beloved Andromeda. At eleven-thirty, she threw back the coverlet, wrapped a black shawl around her shoulders, and moved silently down the hallway to the back staircase. At the rear door she hesitated, certain that she would be heard, even with the chorus of late-summer crickets that filled the night.

To her relief an uproar erupted among the gaggle of geese that roamed the yard. It wasn't unusual for fights to break out among them. Their honking at such times was loud enough to mask any metallic click of the backdoor latch.

Good, she thought.

Almira stepped over the threshold and into the night. As she closed the door behind her, she slipped a scrap of material into the mechanism, hoping it would muffle the noise of the latch when she returned.

On the back step she put on a pair of cloth slippers and drew her shawl overhead like a cowl, then walked off toward the orchard, a dark shadow gliding across the yard. On the way, she passed the privy and carriage house. The half full moon shed enough light for her to see the newly whitewashed outbuildings yet kept her concealed in her dark clothing.

She stepped along the lane and turned at the path leading into the orchard. Sandborne's old dog came up, happily wagging his tail and panting. Daniel must be near—he had to be. A voice called her through the darkness.

"Mirie. Mirie, I'm over here."

All at once, she and Daniel were face to face and fell into each other's arms.

"Is it really you?" he asked. "I was so afraid you'd already be gone for Albany, or that you wouldn't come at all."

"Oh no, Danny, no. I couldn't wait to see you."

The young pair broke into a frenzy of kisses.

"Do you think anyone knows you're here?"

"No, they're all asleep," Almira said.

"Will you ride out to the lake with me?"

"I'll go anywhere with you, you know that."

Smiling at her answer, he took her hand and led her to Marcus, mounted, and pulled her up in front of him, side-saddle, with her arm around his waist.

"Hold on tight," he said, as they trotted off into the night.

Soon they were at their favorite place again, sitting side by side on the rock ledge, holding hands and talking quietly about all that had happened over the previous two weeks. Almira told him about the terrible argument with her father. "That old man said things that'll be hard to forget."

"I'm very sad for the way this has gone," Daniel said. "In all the years I've known your father, I've never seen him so angry. It's all my fault. I should have spoken to him first, but—"

"Don't feel that way. We haven't done anything wrong."

They kissed again. She described her conversation with Sandborne and their system of secret signals.

"Bless his heart," Daniel said. "I don't know how we could have seen each other without his help."

Almira cocked her ear to the lake. "Listen," she said. "Do you hear that?"

"I do." He pointed into the darkness. "Look there, can you see the sparks from the funnel and the light on her bow? I think she's the Vermont, on her way to Plattsburgh."

"Sandborne told me you were working on the Burlington. I waited here every day to see if the steamship would come by."

Daniel's face lit up. "Every time we passed by this place, I looked for you too. Last week I was sure I saw you waving your straw hat from this very ledge. I called out to you, but you couldn't hear me." He clasped her hands in his. "Now we are here together."

"But Danny, Father tells me I leave Monday. What'll we do then? I won't be back for months, maybe not until next summer."

Daniel looked at her sad face. "I've thought a lot about this. I think I have a plan," he said. "You go on to Albany. I'll follow you there. I don't yet know how, but I'll find some work with daguerreotypes. Maybe I'll have to go to New York or Philadelphia, I don't know, but I'll learn the profession and become a daguerreotypist while you're at the academy. In Albany, we can see each other if we're careful. I'll make a success of it. That is my pledge, and someday we'll be married before your father can prevent it."

The moments which followed underscored the gravity of what was said. They'd sat like this before, except this time it was dark, and there were a million crickets around them, witnessing their words, chirping in unison.

Daniel placed his hands at her elbows. "I must ask you directly, Miss Hamilton. Will you be my wife? Because if you will, I am prepared to dedicate my life to you."

"Yes, Mr. Dwyer," she said. "I will proudly be your wife."

They kissed again and again. In the knowledge that their remaining moments were slipping away from them, each kiss took on a growing desperation new to their love.

Daniel and Almira sank to the bed of damp, lush clover behind them, their frenzied kisses driven by a craving to be in contact in every way possible.

"I love you so much," she said, her voice breathless. "Don't ever leave me."

"No, never."

Almira pulled herself across Daniel's powerful chest. Bolder than she would have ever imagined, she found a new way to kiss him again. Their desire ignited and could only be satisfied in one way. Through her petticoats, she felt the firm breadth of him underneath, and something more. She needed Daniel. She felt born to need him and wait for him as the flower awaits the honeybee.

In each other's arms, they flattened the clover together. First this way, then that. The heavens were displayed above them. This, she thought, must be what people meant by star gazing.

At that very moment the most brilliant shooting star she'd ever seen, streaked across the sky. It must be a sign, she thought.

"Go ahead," she said, and kissed his ear.

"What?"

"Make me yours. Take me."

"But it's wrong. We're not married."

She reached down and took him in her hand.

"Mother of God, Mirie. Touchin' me like that, I won't be able to stop."

"Don't try to stop," she whispered. "Make me yours. Take me." Instinctively, Almira placed her heels to his back. "Make love to me as you would your wife."

The night air was filled with the scent of Daniel's woolen clothing, lush, damp grass and earth. Marcus stood nearby grazing while crickets and a whip-poor-will called from the trees.

Having been up the entire night, Almira tried to eat her morning meal quietly. Thoughts of her secret rendezvous with Daniel filled her mind. Directing it toward anything else was an effort.

Loretta's idle conversation had long grown tedious when Hamilton folded up his newspaper and interrupted. "Almira," he said. "I have something to tell you which may not be pleasing."

The sound of his voice made her heart beat wildly, and the color drained from her face. Terrifying thoughts raced through her head. Was she found out? Had her father somehow discovered her and Daniel's midnight tryst? Had what they had done together manifested itself on every feature of her face?

"Yes, Father," Almira whispered. "What is it you wish to tell me."

"I'm sorry, but I will not be in a position to accompany you to Albany tomorrow. Some business affairs have emerged which require I remain here in Willsborough."

Almira squeezed her eyes shut. She felt dizzy and gripped the edge of the table. Her relief was tremendous. "Oh, no," she sighed, though the action was disingenuous. "What shall I do?"

"We anticipated your disappointment, my dear," Loretta said reassuringly. "But your father and I would not have you travel unescorted under any circumstance."

"Of course not," affirmed Hamilton. He took a long drink of coffee and began his instructions. "When you take the steamer in the morning you will meet with a business associate of mine from Plattsburgh, a Mr. Nelson Platt. His daughter is also beginning studies at the Albany Female Academy. He's escorting her to Albany, and therefore you will travel with them."

"They'll accompany me aboard the packet boat as well?"

"Yes, and I've taken care that you will be aboard the same one as before."

"The *Empress.*"

"That's correct," said Hamilton, resuming his instructions. "When you reach Albany, Platt will deliver you and your trunks to the home of a certain Mrs. Bright. She keeps a boarding house for academy girls like yourself."

"Susannah Platt is a lovely young lady," said Loretta. "I think you two will be fast friends."

"You are acquainted with her?" Almira asked.

"Oh yes. Susannah is a bit younger than you, if I remember correctly, but she is a sweet girl."

Of course, she thought, Father and this...woman, knew each other from Plattsburgh. But how well, and for how long?

That afternoon, hoping to ride Ginger Snap for what would surely be the last time that year, Almira called on Sandborne to fetch the pony. Mounting at the granite stepping block, she rode past the garden where Sally and Julia were gathering ripe muskmelons. Along the familiar trail she continued, past the orchard, noticing how comfortable and confident she felt sitting side saddle. Daniel has taught me well, she thought, but then, he is the son of one of Her Majesty's Lancers.

The promontory, with its familiar rock ledge and copse of trees, was just ahead. Almira hurried her pony to where she and Daniel had lain only a few hours before. Here, she looked down on their bed of clover. It was matted and trampled. If she were to lay down, she hoped she might feel the lingering impression of their bodies. She dismounted and let Ginger Snap's reins free, knowing the pony wouldn't wander far.

Once on her back, the impression of her shoulders felt distinct and familiar. Almira closed her gray eyes. She thought back to the press of Daniel against her. Last night, he'd set off something left unfinished and unsatisfied. Trying to summon more of what she'd felt then, she slipped a hand into the pocket of her dress. She moved silently and deliberately, concealed under yards of petticoats. Desperate to reproduce his touch, her hand mimicked Daniel's gentle caress. She probed deeper, raising one knee. With a quickening rhythm, her breathing coming harder, faster, she released a cascade of pleasure. Almira's body shuddered in ways that were new and wonderful. Her eyes opened briefly but remained unfocused. She closed them again, clenched tightly against each successive wave. She bit her gloved fist and gasped as another washed over her, then another, until they gently subsided. Breath slowing, she opened her eyes. Almira realized she was gazing toward the path into the trees where she hadn't dared go since her mother's death.

Every time she would explain that she needed to mourn alone, so heavy was her grief. It wasn't a lie, exactly, but since that day Almira couldn't bring herself to enter the copse of trees. She would sit at the nearby rock ledge instead. Sometimes Daniel had joined her and they would share stolen kisses.

How things had changed. Almira sat up and wiped the tears from her face. She rose and made her tentative way to the pathway. It meandered through the trees to a familiar clearing. In the center stood the three tiny markers for her sister and brothers; a miniature cemetery for children, to which a large headstone of white marble had been recently added.

She approached slowly. Gloriana Olcott van Elst, wife of George Washington Hamilton. Born August 8, 1801, died October 12th, 1840.

This private and protected place, where all her lost children might play through eternity, was her mother's idea. Expecting to weep, cry, or feel the ache of separation somehow amplified, Almira waited, but nothing came. Nor did she feel her mother's rebuke. In truth, she felt nothing at all.

Almira turned her back to the graves. From within the deep shade, she beheld the lake and mountains displayed in their sunlit glory. It was a sort of theater, this place, with trees framing the panorama the way curtains of a stage would.

The stone bench beckoned, a place to commune with memories of the departed. Almira took a seat. There was room for two.

Wouldn't it be nice, she thought?

Under the weight of it all she lay down on the cool stone and, as if laying her head on her mother's lap, fell asleep.

In the morning, with Loretta's help, she finished the last of her packing, including a basket with toiletries, a book to read, and some fried chicken.

With all her preparations complete, Almira went out to the paddock where Ginger Snap and the other horses were kept. Her pony ambled to the fence, anticipating the little green apple that Almira held out. As she fed Ginger Snap the treat, Sandborne came by and stood beside her, observing how gently she petted the horse's nose.

"Don't be worried, miss," he said. "I will see to it that she's taken good care of."

Almira wiped a tear from her eye, surprised at her sudden display of emotion. "Sandborne, I will miss you. You have been as a grandfather to me my entire life."

"Thank you, miss. That's very kind of you, but soon you'll return, and I'll be here as you left me, the same old sixpence, so don't be sad."

On her way back to the house she scooped Wigwam up with one hand under his chest and scratched his head with the other. "Ah, my little lion," she said. "You and I have been such good friends, haven't we? Now listen closely. I will be going away for a while, but I will soon return, I promise." She set him down on the ground and continued her petting. He strutted back and forth under her hand. "You shall be in charge whilst I am away. The estate is under your supervision. Now carry-on Wigwam and do keep the mice away from Momma's things."

Inside, Almira bade an indifferent farewell to Julia, then emerged from the house with a basket on her elbow. Her stepmother, little Egbert, and Sally, holding baby Dorothea, were already waiting at the mounting stone.

Loretta embraced her. "Do write us a letter at least once a week or more often. It should please me very much if you did." She pressed a five-dollar gold piece into Almira's hand and whispered, "Here is something for you if you become homesick. In that case you must take my advice. Go straight away to a milliner and brighten your mood with a new bonnet. It is the only certain remedy I know of."

Almira was surprised at her stepmother's generosity and expressed sincere appreciation. Admittedly, she hadn't always been kind to Loretta and felt sorry the two had not come to know each other better. It was the warmest interchange they had ever shared. Of course, she could never replace Mother, but perhaps they could be friends of a sort after all.

She crouched down and asked for a kiss from Egbert, who threw himself at her open arms.

"Do you promise to take care of Wigwam and Ginger Snap for your big sister?"

Egbert nodded and reached for his mother's hand.

Meanwhile, Hamilton had driven the buggy up from the carriage house. He called for Almira to finish her goodbyes and to get in. If they were to avoid missing the steamboat, it was time to leave.

As they drove off, Almira looked behind at the house with its proud columns and the outbuildings behind it. This was the only home she had ever known.

"Leaving this place will be a good thing for you," Hamilton said after they were underway. "Once you're at the academy, you'll get your mind away from silly ideas. You'll have a new way of thinking about things, one which I think you sorely need."

There was no point in responding. Daniel was following her to Albany, and her father couldn't prevent it.

Hamilton noticed her quiet and frown. "It has been almost a year since your mother's death. I know it's been a very hard time for you. It has been for me too. I hope you know that."

Almira didn't comment. Her face was turned away from him. A steamboat whistle sounded in the distance, and for the first time in months, she felt more sad than angry.

Chapter 25

July, 1971

The archivist at the New York Public Library was a middle-aged man. He had a bow tie and breath laden with the scent of coffee and cigarettes. Bringing a roll of microfilm marked, Census, 1840, Essex County, New York, from the shelves, he demonstrated how to load the reels onto the microfilm projector. "You might have to search around before you find what you're looking for," the archivist told him. "But these old census records can tell you a lot, so it's worth the effort."

He was right. It required perseverance, but in the end, David came away with some solid documentation about the Hamilton household in 1840. It was disappointing—individuals weren't listed by name with specific ages, but a profile of the household did emerge. There were three males; two of them middle-aged, one of whom must have been Hamilton, and one a young adult. The latter, he supposed, was probably Daniel.

There were also three females, one of whom was middle aged. It was impossible to tell whether this older woman was Mrs. Hamilton or Almira's stepmother. There was one young adult female who was no doubt Almira, and one an adolescent, almost certainly the domestic girl.

If he was going to meet Angela, he had to rewind the microfilm spool and gather up his notes.

As they'd agreed on the phone, he stood waiting at the employee's exit when Angela got off work. She came rushing through the door beaming with anticipation over their trip to Shelter Island. Since he had the Ghia with him, the plan was to drive to Fong's for supper.

While he negotiated traffic, she said, "This is gonna be such a gas. I've never been out that far on the island. Tina says the beaches are something else."

"Yeah, well, I have to talk to you about that. I don't think I can go this weekend."

Angela's happy anticipation deflated like air released from a balloon. "What do you mean? I'm all packed and ready."

"I know, and I'm sorry, but the Brimfield antiques fair starts next weekend and I have a ton of stuff I've got to prepare. Maybe we can go some other weekend later in the summer."

Angela's jaw dropped, but only for a moment. "I don't get you. One minute you're all hot and bothered to go see—what the hell was it?" She slapped her forehead. "Oh yeah, paintings of boring people doing boring things, which I agreed to just to keep you happy. Now, all of a sudden you remember you have some antique fair to go to. You only just thought of that now?"

"No, actually I thought of it a couple of days ago."

"And you still came, knowing I was packing and making plans. Isn't that considerate of you?"

"Yeah, well, there was some research I needed to do at the library. I thought maybe we could go somewhere else for tonight."

"What do you mean, research?"

"Some census records about the people who used to live in the house."

"Okay, I get it. You've got time for dead people. You don't have time for me."

"Angie, don't make it sound ugly."

"Ugly? Ugly?" She sputtered with rage. Flecks of spittle flew in David's direction. "You want ugly? Okay, since this was going to be our big beach party you can go pound sand. How do you like that for ugly?"

"C'mon, be cool."

"No. I'm serious. This is bullshit. Let me off at the corner. I'm taking the subway home."

All the way back to Willsboro, David felt lousy. It wasn't right to let Angela down like that. The Fourth of July had a special significance for her. He knew it, but he did it anyway.

Dr. Koenigsberg had once told him, "Remember David, interpersonal events can always be interpreted in terms of moving toward, moving away, or moving against. It's Object Relations, Karen Horney's work. I met her at a symposium in Chicago. She was from Hamburg. Brilliant woman. Very, let us say, dynamic. You should ask me about her some time."

Koenigsberg; all his stories. All his memories. David had some of his own. Like the night he met Angela. He'd had a terrible time after Cheryl Jankowsky's suicide. He was drinking a lot. David remembered sitting at a bar in The Village, alone, chain smoking and drunk. This girl with a long black ponytail and hoop earrings was dancing barefoot in her miniskirt. The soles of her feet were filthy. She had this gooseneck move going on. It made her look ridiculous, but she didn't take herself seriously. It was a quality he envied.

She must have noticed him watching, because she looked up and stared back without missing a beat. They both broke into smiles—hers good enough to make him laugh out loud. As the music ended and a new song started up, she strode directly to him, her forehead beaded with perspiration. Her flushed cheeks and neck were bright red from dancing. She wore a gold necklace with a tiny crucifix attached, like a lot of Catholic girls.

"If you're gonna laugh at me," she said. "Then dance with me too. Come on, I love this song."

What the hell was that song anyway? It didn't matter, except that it marked the start of a happier time. Now things between them were so complicated.

The next night he was startled awake at two a.m. That familiar glow of lamplight from under the door to Almira's sitting room on once again. Legal pad in hand, he knocked a few times and opened the latch. She looked up from her reading and smiled.

"Bonsoir, doctor," she greeted as he stepped in.

David bowed with exaggerated aplomb. *"Bonsoir, Mademoiselle Hamilton."*

"Please do make yourself comfortable," she said, "and tell me how you have been."

David smiled to himself. Almira's self-confidence was amusing.

"I've been well," he said. "What are you reading?"

185

"A copy of Godey's," she said. "It is describing the miniatures made by Mr. Cornelius of Philadelphia. They are unsurpassed."

"Are they?"

"That is what they say," said Almira. "Have you ever had your miniature taken?"

"If you mean a daguerreotype, no, but I do know what a daguerreotype is."

"I thought you might. Few people hereabouts have ever yet seen one. I've had my miniature twice taken. You should sit for yours too. I assure you, it is not in the least painful."

They had a few more minutes of small talk until David raised the subject of her mother. "Would you tell me about her?"

"My mother was kind and gentle," Almira began. "She was loved by all who knew her, but she is gone. Well, she is in a better place. Anyway, so I am told."

In spite of her genteel presentation, David sensed more than sarcasm. He sensed bitterness. "Do you doubt that?"

"No, I suppose not. It only seems so unfair."

"To whom? You or her?"

The question caught Almira off guard. "Unfair to both of us."

"What happened?"

She set her magazine aside. "Mother was sickly for a long time with consumption. The day she passed, I was away. I arrived home too late even to say goodbye."

David noticed a phenomenon he'd seen once or twice before. When challenged, just for a second or two, Almira seemed to move in stop-motion. He called it "strobing," or the "Strobe Light Effect". He took it as a sign of stress.

"Are you feeling alright?" he asked. "Would you prefer to leave the subject alone?"

"No," she said. "Perhaps it is good for me to talk about these things. I've never discussed this with anyone, excepting Daniel."

Almira began drumming her fingers on the sofa cushion, but her lips were pursed like someone refusing to speak. Then she blurted out, "I thought it was quite improper."

"What?" David said. "What was improper?"

"Father's marriage to that woman. It wasn't even a year since Mother's death." Her hands clenched into small fists.

"You're angry about this."

"Yes, I am."

"You feel your father remarried too soon."

"Of course I do."

"How long was it actually?"

"Six-and-one-half months. Disgraceful."

"I see. How many months should it have been? Twenty, twenty-five? Thirty-five?"

Almira dodged the question. "She is not like Mother. She has intemperate habits."

"I understand that," David countered. "She isn't your mother, but is it reasonable for you to have expected her to be?"

"No, I suppose not," she said grudgingly, unhappy to be challenged.

David's psychotherapy training dictated he humanize the object of her anger.

"Tell me about your stepmother."

"She is a widow from Plattsburgh." Almira took another deep breath. "She brought her two children with her."

"A widow," David observed. "That might have been a difficult thing for—what was her name?"

"Loretta."

"Thank you. It must have been difficult for Loretta to have her husband pass away."

"Yes, I imagine it could have been."

"You've spoken about how terrible it was when your mother died. Could Loretta's pain have been similar to yours?"

Almira shifted position on the daybed, scanned the room, and changed the subject. "Doctor, have you seen Wigwam?"

David supposed she'd gone as far as she would tonight, and he wasn't expecting any more.

Suddenly, Almira spoke out. "I ought to have been nicer to Loretta, yet I wasn't. That was wrong of me."

"Why, what happened.?"

"When she and Father married, I was very upset with her, but not only her." Her words sounded carefully considered. "I was angry about so many things at the time. It was all I could think about."

"And if you hadn't been preoccupied with your anger, what would your thoughts have been about?

"What do you mean?"

"Well," said David, "I'm wondering if your anger toward Loretta was intended to distract you from something more disturbing."

Almira drew in her chin and directed her attention to another corner of the room, pondering the question. "I cannot now say, doctor. Perhaps later I can."

Her image flickered, stabilized, flickered again, then disappeared.

A few weeks went by. David called twice, but both times Tina answered and told him Angela wasn't in. "No," she said, "I don't know where Angela is. And no, I don't know when she'll be back."

David knew she must be angry. She had every right to be. Sending an apologetic letter would be the decent thing to do, but he kept putting it off and ultimately didn't send anything. In truth, he liked this distillation of his life into a few basic elements—eat, sleep, think about Almira.

Chapter 26

August, 1841

At the Willsborough docks the *Burlington* lay waiting, taking on or discharging passengers and cargo as the case dictated. Almira felt exhilarated at the chance Daniel might still be a crewmember and aboard. While she scanned the deck for the faintest sign of her beloved, a pair of boys took her trunks onto the vessel.

Hamilton hailed a well-dressed gentleman about his own age standing on the deck with a teen-aged girl. The men on a first name basis, greeted each other and introduced their daughters.

She'd hoped the girl from Plattsburgh would be less childlike, but Susannah was a gangly, red haired girl of about fourteen, with traces of awkward childhood still showing in her features and movements. Her skirts were a bit short, with ankles peeking out from underneath her petticoats, as if she'd grown a few inches overnight.

"I'm so happy we are traveling together." Susannah's tone bubbled with excitement. "I've never been to a true city and have no idea of what to expect."

For the first time in her life, Almira felt sophisticated and experienced. "Allow me to be your guide," she said with reserve.

The two conversed politely, but Almira kept looking past her new companion for some sign of Daniel.

The whistle blew a warning for all who were not passengers to leave the steamer. Hamilton broke off his conversation, stepped up to his daughter, and folded her close. He took a half step back and placed

189

his hands on her shoulders. "I will be coming to Albany on business sometime in the coming month. In the meantime, my girl, I expect you to do three things. Attend to your studies, take care not to overdraw your allowance, and at all times give a good account of our family's name. Am I clear?"

"Yes, Father," she said.

Hamilton pressed her to his shoulders once more. Almira felt him swallow back tears. "Now write to us as soon as you have arrived. And remember always that your father loves you deeply."

Almira had never before seen him make a public display of affection. Hamilton turned, shook Nelson Platt's hand, and quickly left the boat.

"Don't worry about a thing, George," Platt called after him. "Your daughter is in good hands."

Once the ship was under way the trio made their way to the bow, where there were some comfortable benches situated. Mr. Platt sat on one and picked up a copy of the *Buffalo Commercial* lying on the seat. Almira and Susannah sat together, talking. It seemed clear that Daniel was no longer on the *Burlington*. Almira's consoled herself with the fact it might mean he was already on his way to Albany.

True, her hopes were deflated, but the Plattsburgh girl would provide some distraction during the journey. They compared features of their lives, siblings, of which Susannah had four older brothers. They both had a cat at home, and they shared a mutual admiration for the novels of Mrs. Sedgwick. The girls were discussing their favorite titles when Platt's gravelly voice interrupted.

"My good God. The steamboat Erie burned and sank at Buffalo. It says here over one-hundred and seventy-five people were killed. Susannah, are you listening?"

"Yes, sir."

Without raising his head, Platt read aloud. "So rapidly was the spread of the flames, that in five minutes the whole boat from stem to stern was enveloped, and the passengers and crew forced overboard, or surrounded by the fire and literally burnt alive." Mr. Platt looked up at the two. "Can you imagine?"

Almira's new friend looked alarmed by the news. "Don't be worried," she told Susannah. "I've traveled on this steamboat before and know it to be of the safest variety, with a most competent crew."

"I must confess, I am a little frightened." Susannah looked toward her father, who was again concealed behind his newspaper. "But more about starting at the academy than of this steamship exploding."

"Don't be apprehensive," Almira said. "The academy is a beautiful building and Principal Crittenden a learned yet genial man."

"But what will the other girls be like. That's what worries me. In Plattsburgh, they tease me for being awkward, which I know I am."

Almira patted her hand. "I'm sure they'll welcome us. And remember, we may be the only lake girls at the academy, but we will not be the only new scholars."

As the steamboat neared Whitehall, Almira thought more and more about Sarah Rawson. Their brief time together on the *Empress*, and the few letters they'd exchanged since, had awakened Almira's need for an older sister to whom she could turn for mature advice. In comparison to their womanly friendship, Susannah seemed all the more childlike. How much Almira wished she'd had a chance to send Sarah a letter. Had she known she would be in Whitehall this day, they might have visited, if only for a few minutes.

At their destination Almira hoped she might yet catch sight of Sarah or Ezra Rawson. She didn't, but she did see the Empress among a half dozen other canal boats, already secured to the loading dock.

They waited among baggage and cargo for their packet to be loaded. Once the call went out that the *Empress* was ready, the passengers went aboard. A few minutes later, Almira stood on the deck of the packet again. It felt good. The crew were unfamiliar, but Captain Thorne was immediately recognizable by his straw top hat. Leading her companion through the rear deck and into the main cabin, Almira reminded her to watch her step.

A privacy curtain blocked the entrance way leading to the ladies' cabin. Inside two women sat close together in a corner. One of them held an infant in her arms.

"I'm Marie Hart," said the one wearing black. "And this is my sister, Carolina Ashmore."

After introducing themselves, Almira leaned over and said, "You have a beautiful baby."

"Her name is Ruth," the mother said.

A pair of young, barefoot hoagies appeared in the cabin entrance, carrying trunks and bandboxes. Almira held out two large penny coins. "You may stow the cowhide trunk in this locker. And all of us would appreciate your cleanest pillows tonight, or at least a fresh napkin to rest our heads upon."

"Yes, ma'am," one of the boys said with a salute. "We'll see that you ladies are taken care of smartly."

After the boys left, the women thanked Almira for her generosity and foresight. "We're going to join our husbands," the sisters explained. "They have bought farms in Illinois, in Coles County."

"My goodness, you have a long journey," Susannah said.

"Yes, we do." Marie looked to her companion. "But my sister and I don't know the traveler's ways. We've never left our homes in Vermont before, and we're supposed to go by steamboat all the way from Buffalo to Chicago."

"And now," interjected Carolina. "We hear all around of the loss of the steamboat Erie. We're frightened to be on the Great Lakes."

The packet lurched, stopped, lurched again. Through the open windows, orders for the mules to pull could be heard. They were on their way. When Captain Thorne announced his customary speech about the rules of the packet, Susannah joined her father and the other new passengers at the aft deck to listen, but Almira considered herself a seasoned canal traveler, so she remained talking with the sisters. Having only just removed the last of her own full-mourning adornments, she noticed Marie was dressed entirely in black.

"You are in bereavement."

Mrs. Hart, who was tickling her sister's baby with a fingertip, stopped. "Yes, my own newborn daughter. It's not been but three months since."

"I am sorry. Forgive me."

"Thank you," said Marie. "The hardest for me was to leave her in her little grave in Wallingford. I wanted to take her with me, but my husband said it was better to leave her buried where she is."

"Now you're beginning a new life on the prairie," Almira said, trying to sound encouraging.

"Yes, we shall see how it goes."

During the evening meal pork chops and potatoes, followed by apple pie were served out. Once again flies were a constant nuisance. Yet the food was good, so said the Vermont farmer's wives as they ate unselfconsciously from their knives.

With the meal finished, the sisters excused themselves, retiring to the ladies' cabin. The rest of the passengers went outside. Most of the men climbed to the roof, but Susannah and Almira took seats on the rear deck.

Twilight brought an end to the day. A thick mist rose from the canal, obscuring everything beyond the towpath. The air damp and clammy the girls gathered their shawls closer, but the materials were too light to keep them warm. They got up and curtseyed toward the crewman standing at the rudder.

"Goodnight steersman," Almira said.

"Good night ladies." He touched a hand to his cap and nodded in return.

In the dining salon the table had been taken away and all the men's bunks unfolded from the wall. Almira and Susannah walked past the water closet and galley, then parted the curtain and stepped into the ladies' quarters. They were surprised to find Marie nursing her sister's baby.

"Oh," they said in unison. "Excuse us."

Marie looked up with a wan smile. "No, please stay. My sister was almost done with our Bible reading."

Carolina cleared her throat. "Fear thou not; for I am with thee: be not dismayed; for I am thy God: I will strengthen thee; yea, I will help thee; yea, I will uphold thee with the right hand of my righteousness."

When she finished reading, Carolina put away the Bible and reached out for her baby, who was becoming fussy.

The ladies had started loosening their dresses, preparing to retire for the night, when Almira noticed that Susannah's hair had been arranged in a French braid which hung to her shoulders. It was another of her adolescent and unsophisticated affectations.

"Susie," she said. "Would you like me to arrange your hair more in keeping with your age?"

"You would do that for me?"

"I would." She instructed Susannah to take a seat on one of the lockers. She took a napkin from her basket and pinned it closely around the girl's neck.

Standing behind, the first step was to unbraid Susannah's hair. She found it coarse and unruly. Almira reached into her basket and withdrew a small bottle of scented hair oil. Over and over, she brushed it in, combing the red hair until every stubborn strand had relaxed, darkened and shone like buffed copper.

"Mother and father don't understand that I'm not a little girl anymore," Susannah said. "I'm a young lady and should be allowed to dress accordingly. Wouldn't you agree?"

Almira studied her dispassionately. She wasn't very pretty, the poor girl, but she was supremely sincere. "Tell me. Do you already have the nature of a woman?"

"Yes, for nearly a year." Susannah nodded vigorously, dislodging wiry hairs as she did so. She licked a finger, then pressed them back in place.

The Vermont sisters watched closely as Almira took a comb and made a severe part from left to right, just behind Susannah's ears. She then took the hair at back and twisted it into a tight knot, securing it with a hair pin. "With your color hair, an ebony or dark tortoise comb would look very nice."

"I have only this horn comb," said Susannah, sounding apologetic. "It's very plain, and you're right, it does not show my color well."

Almira didn't comment but parted the hair at the top of Susannah's head along the center, dividing each side into three equal parts as if she were about to braid them. Instead Almira wetted each and, together with strips of brown paper, wound each closely and secured the coil with a hairpin.

"When we unpin it in the morning, you'll have very fashionable curls."

Squeaking with joy, Susannah said, "Oh, thank you so very much." She made to get up, but with one finger Almira held her in place.

"Stay as you are. We're not finished with you yet."

Almira took a pair of tweezers from her basket and went to work plucking outlying eyebrow hairs, of which there were quite a few. When finished she stepped back and regarded her work.

Carolina reached behind her head and pulled out a comb as dark as her hair was long. Blonde coils tumbled down her back to the locker on which she sat. "Here, take this one for yourself," she said.

"I couldn't. Yours is so much nicer."

"Go on, it's only a comb, and I have another." Carolina braided her thick tresses at an astounding speed. "If you like, we can trade. I'll take your old horn comb as a keepsake of our voyage together."

Carolina stood and stepped up behind Susannah. She worked the long teeth of her comb through the knot, securing it in place. "There, don't it look dandy?"

Susannah lavished everyone with appreciation. "Thank you all so much. I'll look so much better, so much more...womanly when we arrive in Albany."

"Tell us," asked Marie. "Why ever do you girls need to go to school? Can't you already read and cypher?"

"We can," Almira said. "But our studies will be about literature and mathematics and philosophy."

"Lands." Carolina's look betrayed her surprise at the curriculum. "My husband says a woman with a head full of schooling is heavy company. Whatever do you need to know those things for?"

"To better our important role as wives and citizens of the republic."

"And to find wealthy husbands," joked Susannah. They all laughed at the thought.

Little Ruth began to stir.

"Might I hold her for a moment?" Almira asked.

Marie held her out. Almira took the child and bounced her gently in her arms. Ruth blew bubbles of spittle.

With a mother's intuition, Carolina said, "You look right at home holding a baby."

Chapter 27

August, 1971

David cranked the paper in his typewriter up and read what he'd written.

> "8/5/71: Death of mother a significant point of trauma/conflict. Hostility toward stepmother disproportionate and contrived. Suggestive of displacement defense mechanism. Possible sexual competition? Explore further."

Clinical notes were important. David had always taken pride in his, but tonight he was dissatisfied. Why? What he'd written didn't sound much different than other clinical notes he'd kept over the years—sex, aggression, interpersonal conflict, the usual stuff. Maybe that was the problem.

Almira was responsive and could be influenced, as any living person in psychotherapy might be, but she was long deceased, as the memorial hanging above his desk made abundantly clear. That surely had treatment implications. Yet the clinical notes he read seemed to avoid the subject or treat it as irrelevant, like one more incidental fact of life.

The idea made him feel cornered. Angela had once said, "You can't believe in ghosts and not believe in God." But if these notes were an accurate description of reality, and if those same notes accepted Almira as real, then there was only one rational conclusion.

David pulled his thoughts back. The conclusion felt immense, overwhelming. Later he could walk out to the lake. Think. Get used to the idea. But for now, one thing at a time. Almira's psychotherapy.

Late the following night, David sat in conversation with Almira. Engrossed in the petit-point braces she perpetually sewed, she seemed at ease and relaxed, though, as was typical, she avoided looking in David's direction. Instead, Almira kept her eyes focused on her needlework.

Though these conversations had been taking place for many months, David still marveled to be speaking with—to be in the living presence of—the person depicted in the daguerreotype portrait displayed in the adjoining room.

This might be a good time to raise the question of her mother's death again.

"I know it is difficult, but I'd like to talk with you a little more about your mother. Would that be all right?"

"Yes," she said. "What would you wish to know?"

"Well, I've been wondering what your earliest memories of her were."

Without interrupting her rhythm of inserting the needle through the canvas and drawing the floss through, Almira spoke. "Oh goodness. I should think her instructing me in needlework." She stopped and raised an index finger. "No, there is something before that. I remember how distraught she was when my sister and brothers died. She cried for weeks. After that, she wore only black for years."

"What happened to them?" David asked.

"The Fell Destroyer took them within a few days of each other," Almira said. "It was horrible how they suffered. I was ill with it too, but for some unknown reason I was spared."

David didn't quite understand.

"Are you not familiar with the term, doctor? I know it only by that name. The throat becomes inflamed. It becomes swollen, making it impossible to swallow or breathe. Before long, one succumbs from lack of air."

Suffocation. He considered what disease she could be describing. Returning to her mother, David asked, "Did their deaths change her? In the way she acted?"

"Mother was never the same." Almira resumed her embroidering. "She sealed their bedrooms closed, toys and all, and forbad anyone to disturb a thing. Soon afterwards she started to be sickly herself."

"You said she had consumption, is that right?" David asked, seeking confirmation of his earlier notes.

"That is correct. She slowly weakened, and it finally took her, but not before we had a few happy years together." Drawing the floss to the back of the canvas, she trimmed it clean and said, "She taught me all I know about needlework."

Finally, David felt ready to probe deeper. "Now," he said, "last time we talked about her, you told me you were gone when she passed. You were away in Albany at the academy?"

Almira, who had begun threading a new color of floss to her needle, stopped short. "No." She spoke slowly, "I was here."

"You were here?" said David. "I'm sorry, but I'm confused."

She didn't answer him or explain but remained quiet for a long time. "Is it necessary we talk about this?"

"I think so, yes. It is part of the talking treatment to help you feel better." He took a risk to say this. First, because she was offering strong resistance, and secondly because he explicitly made a reference to their conversations as a therapeutic process. She would either refuse the premise, in which case any real psychotherapy would be at a standstill for the present or accept it and continue.

"Very well," she said. "If you must know, I was taking a riding lesson."

"With Daniel?"

Again, Almira remained quiet, but David held himself until she spoke.

"Yes," she said very quietly.

"And when you got back here your mother was gone?"

"You don't understand. Mother was unwell for so long a time. She would sleep much of the day. She urged me to go. How was I to know she was so ill?"

From her defensive response, David knew he'd struck a chord. One of their first conversations, in which she'd spoken of being unworthy of forgiveness, came rushing back. Why hadn't he listened? But it's hard to listen when one's ears aren't open, and at the time, questions of forgiveness didn't jibe with his assumptions. He'd been fixated on a psycho-sexual interpretation, which had appealed to him personally but didn't accurately represent her problem.

David now supposed Almira felt tremendous guilt at being absent when her mother died, and even held herself in some way responsible. If this were so, his prior Freudian theory was debunked. Feminine competition with her stepmother wasn't the source of her anger and depressed mood—instead it was guilt and shame.

To test this idea, he provoked her. "Then you had no chance to say a final goodbye because you were out riding with Daniel."

"No." She snapped at him. "I have already told you it was too late. Why do you hector me with these cruel questions?"

Almira's manifestation began to strobe. This was normally a sign that she and the things she brought with her would vanish within seconds. David wanted, above all, for the session to continue and end with her in an enlightened state, not one of deeper entrenchment. He had to say something to salvage the conversation. "Please, Miss Hamilton, try to calm yourself. I didn't mean to upset you."

Her form started to stabilize. Almira sat with her hands still holding her needlework on her lap. Her cast down eyes and weary face wore an expression of deep sadness. A tear ran down her cheek and spattered on the back of her hand. "She begged me to stay, but I told her there was no time. I never thought it would happen so quickly." Almira covered her eyes with one hand and wept.

David allowed her to feel the cathartic discharge of emotion. In fact, he felt her sadness too. That, he knew, was a sign of countertransference intruding on the therapeutic process. *Don't let that happen,* he reminded himself. *Stay dispassionate, keep your emotional distance at all times.*

"It was impossible for you to know when your mother would be called away," he said quietly. "None of us can ever predict these things."

"But I was selfish," she murmured. "I thought only of myself, and now I regret it so."

"You feel guilty that you were not with her."

"Yes."

"Had it been different, what would you have said to her?"

"I would have stayed with her and told her how much I loved her while I could still do so."

David offered a correction. "You mean, how much you still love her. Your love continues, doesn't it?"

Almira nodded.

"And what else would you have said?"

"I would tell her that I'd be lost without her."

A seminar he'd once attended came to mind, a demonstration by Fritz Perls, the originator of Gestalt therapy. David saw this as a perfect opportunity to try one of the techniques. "Tell her as if she were here."

Almira hesitated, perplexed by his direction. "What do you mean?"

Getting up from where he sat, David stepped off to one side. "Let's imagine your mother is sitting on that empty chair. Speak to her."

"I don't think I can do that," Almira stuttered. "It would be silly."

"Sure you can. Go ahead," he said, coaching her along. "Make believe. It's easy."

After a long pause, she swallowed and began speaking. "Mother, I'm sorry I wasn't there with you at the end. I wanted to be there—I really did. Please believe me. I couldn't know." Her voice faltered and stalled. She looked toward David, who nodded encouragingly.

"Go on, you're doing great," he whispered. "What else?"

"I was so selfish that day, and now I miss you so much." Almira stalled, almost as if she was unable to utter more.

"Don't stop," said David. "Continue. Keep speaking to her."

"Mama, it torments me to think you might be angry or feel betrayed. Could you ever forgive me?"

Almira looked up again. This time her eyes were wet with tears, but there was also the faintest smile on her face. Her apparition flickered, and then regained solidity.

"Would you like to rest now?" Weis David said gently.

"No," she said. "I have more to tell." Almira wiped her eyes, straightened her back and took a deep breath. "Mother," she said to the empty chair. "I want you to know that I've become a woman through your example. You have shown me how. With your guidance I've come to know love. You know with whom, and I only wish you could have seen me and Daniel together, so happy, just the way I remember you and Father. Now I know your joy."

She glanced in David's direction. He smiled and she continued. "I'm sorry I couldn't resist love's call when you needed me. Yet somehow, I think...no, I am quite sure you understand."

Pride surged through David. His fragile patient had proven to be so much stronger than he could have guessed. "You've worked hard today. It's time for you to rest."

"Thank you, Doctor Weis," said Almira with a sniffle. "This has been a most peculiar conversation. I feel exhausted, but I feel relieved of a burden as well."

"It pleases me to hear you say that," David said, his voice full of anticipation. "Does this mean you feel at rest?"

He could see Almira's brow furrow as her attention turned inward.

"At rest?" She sighed. "No, It's too late. At rest is a privilege I've squandered. I've thrown it away."

"We can talk about that sometime, if you like."

"In truth, it frightens me to hear you say that Dr. Weis, for there's yet more which could be said if only I have the courage." Almira began restoring the tools of her needlework to the embroidery basket. Her image started to disappear, but as it did, she said, "For now, everything must be put away. Everything must be in its place."

Alone now, David sat in darkness, for the lights she brought with her were gone as well. It took some time to feel grounded again in conventional reality. By then a faint glow to the east was signaling that the sun would soon crest over the mountains across the lake. For the present it was still hidden.

He got up to leave but took one last look into the Quiet Room before he closed the door. It was tranquil, calm, peaceful.

Downstairs, David made a pot of coffee. He sat at his desk and switched on the typewriter. Was this really it? Had Almira reached some endpoint? Probably not. Judging by her remarks, she wasn't fully at rest, even though she clearly reached some therapeutic milestone.

Did a therapeutic milestone mean she wouldn't appear again? Some patients were like that—they can go only so far and then drop out of sight. The thought that she might do the same provoked a wave of anxiety. David wanted desperately for her to return, for in truth he'd fallen in love with her. She'd changed him without intention, simply by being.

It wasn't his habit to cry, but the impulse seized David before he could resist. A wave of sadness a twinge of panic. He felt as he imagined a child might, separated from someone they loved. The overall effect was one of being unanchored. Once unleashed, emotions could run wild, and when carried off, the consequences were hard to predict.

David wiped his eyes and loaded a fresh sheet of paper into the typewriter.

Clinical Notes: August 16, 1971

Patient engaged in empty chair exercise with mother. Reports catharsis of guilt over her death. Also hints at deeper unresolved issues.

Proper formulation of any therapeutic process required concentration, but David's thoughts were too adulterated with emotion, too disorganized for that. A coherent interpretation of events would have to wait. He turned off the typewriter.

David refilled his mug and brought it outside, where he sat on the steps between the Doric columns. He looked around. It was full daylight now. A soft breeze played across the yard. Birds sang in nearby trees. Meanwhile, a pair of crows reported like sentinels from their outposts on the perimeter of the property. David took it all in. *This really is my home. This place, this time in my life,* he thought. For the first time he felt the desire to share them.

His thoughts shifted to Angela. The disorientation she described after the death of her own mother didn't seem very different from Almira's. Maybe they were more alike than he'd realized. He loved them both, but having them both at once was impractical and impossible. Still, if he could love the one, why couldn't he love the other as well?

On the pretense of fixing a bowl of corn flakes, David went back into the kitchen. Instead, he dialed Angela's number. Her roommate, Tina, picked up.

"Who is this?"

"It's Dave Weis. Is Angela there?"

"Do you know what time it is?"

"It's early, I know. I'm sorry."

Tina didn't answer, but he heard her say, "It's mister excitement. Do you want me to hang up?"

After a long minute, Angela's voice came through the receiver. "Yeah," she said, her voice flat and emotionless. "It's me. What do you want?"

"You."

She probably hadn't expected that answer, but neither did he. Angela laughed him off. "You know, you're really something else."

A receptive hint in her voice encouraged him. "I'm serious. How about I come down? We can have a long talk. I can apologize over

Chinese food. A fried rice apology."

"I don't know. I'm all mixed up."

David feared the long silence would be followed by the buzz of a dead line. He felt a little desperate. "Angela, I really miss you. Is it too late?"

"For Shelter Island? Yes, it is. I've used up all my vacation days and classes start next week."

"No, I don't mean Shelter Island. I mean for us. Is it too late for us?"

There was an audible sigh. "It's not too late, no, but something has to change."

"I get it. We'll talk. C'mon, what do you say?"

No answer was forthcoming, but David thought he could hear Tina whispering something in the background.

"Look," he said. "How does this sound? I come down and we take a jet from JFK to Montreal. Make it a real cosmopolitan weekend. Like a mini-trip to Europe."

"I've told you, I don't have the time. Besides, you speak lousy French."

"Well, maybe I've been practicing."

The house was quiet. Dr. Weis was away again, and with him, many of the other strange, confusing interferences which seemed to be present when he was in the building.

Almira blotted her pen and set aside this latest of a thousand letters. Why neither Sarah nor Rebecca ever answered was a mystery. She went to her daybed to read, picked up The Young Lady's Friend but put it down. Without Dr. Weis, her chambers felt all the more lonely. Just being aware of his presence in the house had become a comfort. Goodness, how she'd grown to expect his visits, and in his absence, how much she looked forward to the time with him.

Dr. Weis helped her to feel more settled. He had taught her that she could have loving memories of her mother without the stabbing guilt she'd endured for so long. He'd also shown her how to put down the burden of anger toward Loretta and her father. Yes, he'd opened her eyes, cast light upon some of the darkness in her heart, but where did this new awareness leave her?

Somehow, being consumed by anger and guilt felt safer. For now, Almira was more aware than ever that she was trapped. Aware that there was a world outside of this room, a place where she was not welcome. Aware that she was excluded from everyone and everything she had ever known.

All these years—for now she knew they must be years—she'd been chained to this rock, waiting. She had waited for a letter from Sarah, or Rebecca. Waited for a lighted taper in Sandborne's window, and above all, waited for Daniel to come for her, as she knew he someday would.

Almira longed to talk to Dr. Weis. His odd questions, hard as they sometimes were to answer, were also a comfort. She went to the doorway, hoping she might draw him to her if he was anywhere near. Almira called out silently from the threshold. No one answered.

It took courage but after some time passed, she stepped gingerly into the hall. Like the blind man who knows the building but sees none of it, Almira made her way a little further. Beyond her rooms every motion called for tremendous concentration, as if making her way through water. Whenever she had tried this before it was exhausting, and this day was no different. Yet, even if much seemed...erased, the essential features of the building were intact.

At the door to Father's and Loretta's room, no one answered. Almira turned away. She descended the staircase, but the ground floor was even more peculiar and dreamlike. A buzz like that of a hornet or bee sounded in her head. It could be felt in the air. It was everywhere, but most piercing in the kitchen, where she pressed her hands to her ears and her body quivered uncontrollably.

Turning away, Almira searched further, but grew more desperate as she did. Where had everyone gone? She went to the parlor. It was empty. She went to her father's office, but it was empty too, excepting one corner, wherein was a desk. Upon it was a small machine bearing all the letters of the alphabet.

On the wall above the desk hung a framed memorial. Her father must have acquired this in memory of her mother. Almira stepped closer to read it.

In loving memory of Almira van Elst Hamilton
Born November 16th, 1822
Died December 21st, 1841
Gone but not forgotten.

Almira gasped, hand to mouth. She fled to the hallway and back up the stairs to her rooms. There she bolted the door shut. With her back pressed against it, she waited for her labored breathing to subside.

Her daybed looked inviting and comforting as a mother's lap. She went to it and laid down, curled into a ball, with her knees drawn up close. Almira gathered her skirts in her hands and cried.

Joseph Covais is the author of the **_Psychotherapy With Ghosts_** series published by New Link, an imprint of Mystic Publishing. Before losing his eyesight, Joe produced precise replica clothing for museums, historic sites, and the movie industry, under the business name New Columbia. He was also an avid collector of antiques—especially photography, hand-sewn clothing, and Civil War militaria.

Today Joe works as a psychotherapist with blind and visually impaired persons. He also teaches psychology classes at Community College of Vermont and St. Michael's College, from which he obtained a Master's Degree in Clinical Psychology in 2003.

Joe published his first book, Battery—the story of the Glider Field Artillery of WWII, based on in-depth interviews conducted with veterans. He welcomes correspondence from readers, through Facebook or through direct email at josephcovaisauthor@gmail.com.

Made in United States
North Haven, CT
12 December 2022

28574425R00124